FUNERAL PLATTER

Also by Greg Ames

Buffalo Lockjaw

FUNERAL PLATTER

STORIES

GREG AMES

002000452630

Arcade Publishing • New York

Arcade Publishing books may be purchased in bulk at special discounts for sales promotion, corporate gifts, fund-raising, or educational purposes. Special editions can also be created to specifications. For details, contact the Special Sales Department, Arcade Publishing, 307 West 36th Street, 11th Floor, New York, NY 10018 or arcade@skyhorsepublishing.com.

Arcade Publishing® is a registered trademark of Skyhorse Publishing, Inc.®, a Delaware corporation.

Visit our website at www.arcadepub.com.

10 9 8 7 6 5 4 3 2 1

Library of Congress Cataloging-in-Publication Data is available on file.

Cover design by Erin Seaward-Hiatt

Print ISBN: 978-1-5107-2581-2
Ebook ISBN: 978-1-5107-2583-6

Printed in the United States of America

For my friends—
past, present, and future

CONTENTS

1

Chemistry | 3
Discipline | 14
Men's Room | 27
The Life She's Been Missing | 30
A Domestic Tyranny | 46

2

Hallie Bang | 63
Is the Vagina Necessary? | 72
Benefactor | 84
I Feel Free | 97
Family Album | 119

3

4

*I am trying to hold in one steady glance
all the parts of my life.*

ADRIENNE RICH

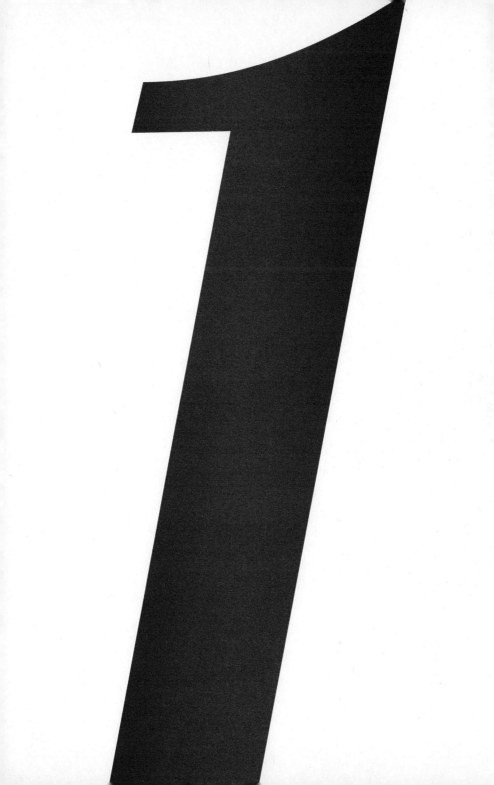

CHEMISTRY

Gretchen arrived first and took a seat by the café's front window. These half-hour coffee dates were a necessary burden since she'd become single again. She refused to waste time with dinner or drinks and kept her expectations low. Life was way too short, she'd told a girlfriend, to fritter away on dudes who couldn't be present: addicts, wounded birds, stockbrokers, wannabe rock stars. No thanks. You could learn a lot about a human being, she believed, over a single cup of coffee.

She kicked her shoes off under the table and continued reading her paperback and barely noticed when a man hurried in, twenty minutes late.

"You Gretchen? I'm Keith," he said, grimacing a little, as if he hated the sound of his own name.

"Nice to meet you," she said and offered her right hand. "Robert has told me a lot about you."

Keith stripped off his leather jacket and sank into the chair opposite her. Sweat stains under his arms darkened the fabric of his dress shirt. "Sorry I'm so late. I got rear-ended a few blocks south of here. I had to, you know, get out, check the damage—there was none, thankfully. But the woman who hit me was really shaken up about it and kind of over apologetic." He laughed. "She wouldn't let me drive away. She kept offering me money."

"How nice," Gretchen said, "that she was so nice to you."

"I waved my hand and told her it was no big deal. These things happen." He smiled at the memory of his own beneficence. "Turns out we went to the same college. And she—"

"Was she hot?" Gretchen said. "Did you get her digits, tiger?"

"Excuse me?" He blinked his eyes three times in rapid succession. "What are you saying?"

"Will you call her up next week to chat about all the *damage* to your *bumper*?"

"I don't think I know what you're talking about." He looked to his left and right, perhaps hoping for corroboration from a witness. "I just had a car accident."

She stared at him but said nothing.

Keith pushed the saltshaker forward with his finger, as though he were moving a pawn on a chessboard, and then he brought it back to its original position beside the pepper. "It wasn't meant as a personal slight, Gretchen."

"I've heard that before." She shoved her book into one of the shoulder bags at her feet. "I see that look in your eye. It's so obvious."

"What are you saying?"

She leaned forward, the points of her elbows on the table. "It's obvious that this just isn't working between us. I don't know what Robert was thinking when he said I should meet you." She stood up and grabbed her coat, almost knocking the chair over in the process.

Heads turned at nearby tables.

Keith reached for her wrist and prevented her from leaving. "Gretchen, please. Give me another chance."

"Oh, Keith, don't," she said and lowered herself into her seat. "Don't. People are looking at us." She allowed him to stroke her knuckles while she averted her eyes.

"Gretchen, listen to me. Let's not throw it all away," he said. "It was just a fender bender." He squeezed her hand. "It happened so fast, and then it was over. I barely even remember her name."

Gretchen shut her eyes and let out her breath. "Did you wear a condom?"

He touched his chest lightly with his fingers. "Look, I would never, ever—Are we still talking about the woman in the other car?"

"There you go again, answering my question with a question. I know that's one of your little tricks to buy time. But your money is no good at this bank. Your chips are expired and the sands have already passed through the hourglass."

Keith shut his eyes and ground his knuckles into the lids. "You're mixing your metaphors."

She glared at him. "So now I'm an idiot?"

He glared back, a muscle flexing in his jaw. "Did I call you an idiot? Did you *hear* me call you an idiot or did you *imagine* it?"

"When was the last time you called me smart?" she asked, her arms crossed on her chest. "When was the last time you made me feel meritorious? Huh? There's a fifty-cent word for you, genius."

Keith turned and took hold of his leather jacket. "I should've known you'd be like this. Everything turns into an argument with you. You're paranoid. And I see you've taken your shoes off in a public place, which is unhygienic, by the way."

"At least I don't iron my blue jeans," she said in a barely audible voice.

"What was that?" His chin jutted forward. "Did you say something?"

"You have no fashion sense, Keith. Look at that braided belt."

He stood up and tried to put on his bomber jacket, but one of the sleeves was turned inside out. "I'm leaving. I knew if I told you about my car accident you'd be like this."

"You knew I'd be like what? What am I like? Inform me."

"You can be so . . ." He shook his head, sat down again across from her. "Damn it, you were right about us. You said it wasn't working out and I didn't want to believe it. I guess I just wanted to hold on because, well—"

"You're scared of being alone?"

"Fine, yes. Because I'm scared of being alone."

Gretchen broke into a grin, moved by his disclosure. "You're so passionate when you're mad, Keith. You have this little vein in your temple. It pulses."

He nodded. "My father was like that, too."

"Good old Papa," she said.

"Dad's been dead eight years now."

"Rest his soul." Gretchen reached across the table and touched Keith's hand. She smiled at him, bringing out The Dimple, one of her best features. "Come on. Put your cool jacket down. Stay. I'll order us two lattés. Just how you like them."

"I don't drink coffee."

"Fine. You can have mango juice, then."

"Don't tell me what I can have and what I can't have, Gretchen. I'm an adult, goddammit. I'm tired of people telling me what to do."

She motioned to a waiter.

"I mean, so what if I never received a hug or a kind word from my father?" Keith looked out the window. "Men of his generation had no access to their emotions. He put me through a good college instead. Isn't that a form of love?"

Gretchen caught the waiter's eye and gestured to him with a tilt of her head. "Mm-hm," she said. "College."

Keith monitored her reflection in the window. "What the fuck was that?"

"What?" Her breath caught in her throat. "What did I do?"

Keith swung his head around to look behind him. "What was that look you just gave him? Are you having an affair with our waiter?"

She cupped her chin in the palm of her hand and looked up at him through her eyelashes. "Did you have a good day doing what you do at work?"

"Answer the question, you deceitful whore."

"Keith, you're jealous of *that* guy?" She nodded in the waiter's direction. "He and I are just old friends. We met while I was waiting for you." She waved at the waiter, but his back was turned.

Keith scooted his chair closer to the table and addressed her in a low voice. "You think you're smarter than everyone with your book, yeah? And the secret looks you make with your face, yeah? But I've got news for you: I'm smart, too, and I see what's happening here." He tilted his head in the direction of the waiter. "I'm going to have words with him. Maybe I'll even invite him out back and settle it like men."

"Suit yourself," she said, "but you'll be sorry."

Keith groaned and covered his face with his hands. "Nobody suffers more than me. This accident with the car and everything. Tax season. My mother's persistence. Stop calling me, Mother." He peeked through his spread fingers. "Oh, she's very warm and sweet, don't get me wrong, Gretchen, you'll love her, but sometimes it's just too much to take."

"I know, I know," Gretchen said, petting the tips of his fingers. "Shhhh. You'll get through it. Here. Play with the salt-shaker again." She thumbed it toward him. "I know how you like that."

"I haven't slept in days. I'm sorry to subject you to this." Keith's hands fluttered at his shirt collar, smoothing the points. "You deserve so much better. I mean, here I am always keeping up this ridiculously handsome exterior. Look at me, everybody. I'm so competent and masculine. It's just bullshit."

"Yup," she said while texting a girlfriend inside her purse, her cell phone hidden from view. "But you're right about one thing: you are a handsome man despite your nauseating personality."

Keith didn't appear to be listening. "And I suppose I created this macho persona for myself as a survival tactic, but it doesn't suit me anymore. I shouldn't be involved with anybody right now. Mother was right. I need to work on myself first. It's not fair to you."

"Don't be so hard on yourself." Gretchen uncapped a tube of vanilla hand lotion and began moisturizing the insides of her wrists. "Fear is a natural reaction to hopelessness. God is dead. North Korea is nuclear. There's a freak show in the White House. But we can lean on others for support."

"Maybe you're right," he said.

"Of course I am. You'll feel better after a nice meal and a big glass of wine. Let's get the fuck out of here."

"Oh, that mouth of yours," he said, browsing the lower half of her face with his narrowed eyes. "Those soft lips. You're a beautiful and strong woman, Gretchen."

Blushing, she looked down and smoothed the napkin across her lap. "Am I?" she said.

"I swear it's true, my love."

She lifted her napkin up, hiding her face so that only her eyes showed. "Am I?" she whispered.

"Jesus, aren't you listening to me? I just told you you are. Why don't you ever listen to me?"

"I wasn't sure I heard you the first time. Relax."

"Well, clean the wax out of your dirty stupid ears."

"You're gonna talk to me about hygiene? You've got filth on your hands, you monster."

He inspected his palms. "I had to check the bumper of my car. Remember my car accident?"

"Was that before you or after you boinked your little college friend?"

The light through the window had shifted. Keith looked at Gretchen, his eyes now assessing every visible inch of her.

She imagined herself as "bathed in dusk" and she leaned back in her chair as though soaking in the tub at home.

"God, you have world-class jugs," he said. "I can't stop staring at your cleavage."

"As long as we're finally being honest," she said, "I'm dying to get my hands on your yogurt knob."

Keith's back straightened, causing his trapezius muscles to expand. "If we weren't in a public place, I would teach that waiter how to honor and respect a woman's cooter."

She nodded in agreement. "And I would ride you straight into a coma."

He beamed with joy for a moment before the weight of reality descended again. "But what's the point of anything?" he said, slumped in his chair. "Soon they'll be cloning us. Genetic engineering. I'm sure you've been reading about it."

"Of course."

"Soon this whole city will be crowded with people who look exactly like us, saying the exact same things to each other. Do you know what that means, my love?"

She nodded. "We'll have to start making reservations in advance."

"This is no joke, goddammit." He thumped his fist down on the table, rattling the water glasses. "No jokes are being told here. Capitalism has failed. Soon we'll be forced to work grueling hours in canning factories for the master race. Enjoy your creature comforts now, you posh layabout, because soon there will be no more cafés. No more lattés."

"You won't hear me crying about it." She flipped her chin defiantly at the espresso machine. "Smash the system."

"Life as we know it will change forever, Gretchen." He lowered his voice. "The government will monitor everything we say, seeking out the dissenters among us. They will implant tracking devices in our brains."

She leaned forward and touched her forehead to his. "Widespread famine. Syphilitic dogs roaming the streets. Et cetera. Of course there will be a revolution."

The word "revolution" seemed to animate Keith. Once again he flexed his neck and shoulders. "I'll spill blood for you, Gretchen. I would die in the streets for you."

"I might be too busy fighting to notice that," she said, "but I will dedicate my first manifesto to you, in memory of you."

Keith cradled her breasts in his hands. "I shall always remember these meaty honkers." He cast a suspicious glance at the waiter. "I don't care if you had sex with that man. We are animals, after all."

"We only held hands and smooched a little. *Avec* tongue."

"It's okay, because I have had this time with you. Remember everything about this, Gretchen. Write it all down. Tell the world what we have done here."

She smiled at him. "You bet."

"And when you see him again, tell Robert I love him like a brother. He was right to introduce us."

"And I am like a sister to Robert. Wait, does that make this incest?"

"It is a love that cannot be contained. Taboos were invented by cowards."

"When you talk tough like that, I get so hot."

"I'm on fire with passion for you, for the revolution, for life itself."

She tore open a packet of sugar and emptied it on the floor, a symbolic gesture that they both understood.

"Yes," he said. "Yes."

They stared at each other across the table, their faces flushed, pupils dilated.

The waiter, a skinny kid with a ponytail and a light starter beard, appeared beside their table. "You guys wanna order anything yet? I didn't want to interrupt. Seemed like you were having a pretty intense chat over here."

Nobody said anything.

The young waiter looked at Gretchen, then at Keith. "Maybe start you guys with something to drink?" He scratched his armpit. Another moment passed in silence. "Tell you what. I'll come back in a few minutes, give you folks a little more time. Sound good?"

"I'll summon you when it's time," Keith told him.

"Cool beans," the kid said and retreated.

Gretchen pushed her chair back and rose to her feet. "We must go now," she said. "They're closing in."

Keith remained seated. "Closing in," he said, deflated.

She shouldered her purse and her other bag. "There's no time left. Come on."

He looked up at her. "No time," he whispered. "No time."

"Get up." She seized his hands and pulled him to his feet. "We have to move on from this place immediately."

"Move," he said, as if he'd never heard the word before.

"I'll die if I have to stay here another second, Keith."

"Okay, yes, right!" he said, snapping to attention. "We have to move right now or we never will."

"You guys ready to order?" the waiter called out from behind the espresso machine.

"Capitalist chump. I don't answer to you." Keith tossed a dollar on the floor and kicked his chair over. "Pick that up, you middle-class slave."

Gretchen did Keith one better. She found a lighter in her purse and set fire to a five-dollar bill. She left it burning on the table. "I killed your God," she said to the waiter. Then she shoved open the glass door and held it for Keith.

It was cold and dark outside. Arms linked, they marched into the street.

Keith leaned over and whispered in Gretchen's ear. "Remind me to thank Robert for introducing us."

"Somehow he just knew," she said. "As if he had inside information."

Abruptly Keith stopped walking, spun Gretchen around and looked into her eyes. "How did Robert know we would get along so well?"

"What are you implying?"

Keith stared at her.

"Robert is such a dear friend," she said, "but he is a bit of a sympathizer."

"He's an apologist, Gretchen. Which is to say, a traitor."

"Unlike you." She kissed Keith on the lips. "You're all man."

Keith wrapped his arms around her. "Robert wants to control everything to avoid thinking about death," he said directly into her mouth, "but he can't control this, can he?"

"He's a major problem," she said. "Maybe we should have a strong word with him. Tonight."

"Are you saying what I think you're saying?"

"Am I? You tell me."

"Let's eat dinner first and then decide."

"Sounds like a plan." Gretchen smiled at him. "I'm so hungry I could eat the spritz from a gobblespark's fadoodle."

Keith threw his arm around her shoulder and kissed her cheek. "I was thinking the exact same thing."

DISCIPLINE

When she was twelve years old, my older sister Cathy carried a ventriloquist's dummy with her wherever she went. The dummy's name was Marilyn, and at first nobody had the heart to tell Cathy that Marilyn was not really a dummy, but was in fact a charred log from our fireplace. But what could we do? Cathy skated freely on the frozen pond of her imagination, and as she wasn't hurting anybody but herself, we generally ignored her eccentricities. Every night she slept in her narrow bed with this splintered wedge of burnt wood. She cuddled with it on the sofa while watching soap operas and sitcoms, and she left ashy smudges on everything she touched, from the refrigerator door to my previously white gerbils. Cathy's homeroom teacher was concerned. The school psychologist, Nancy Palermo, asked my father if we had recently lost any family members to a house blaze or a fiery car crash. My father answered in the negative. Ms. Palermo wanted to see Cathy three times a week after school for private consultations.

We lived in a squat, crumbling, yellow brick house surrounded by tiger lilies. All the houses on Hood Lane were the same size. Our street appealed to young couples just starting out, elderly folks in pajamas, recovering addicts trying to get a fresh start in life one day at a time, and struggling small business owners. There were no block parties or street fairs, but every now and then some drunk kid would crash his father's car into a tree, and we'd all gather around swimming in the headlights.

My mother's absence from our lives—she said she was "just getting her head straight" in Tampa, Florida—forced my father to become the sole nurturer in our household. He hadn't touched a vodka tonic in over fourteen months, but when my mother left for Florida, a move that took us all by surprise, he stopped going to his Don't Drink meetings and stayed home with us.

"The other kids will make fun of you. You don't want that, do you, honey?" he said to Cathy. He unwrapped a lollipop and paced in front of my sister, who was seated on the family room sofa clutching Marilyn to her breast like some horribly burned infant. I sat cross-legged on the floor at Dad's feet, paying close attention because I knew that someday I'd need to write all this down, just in case somebody asked me why I behave the way I do. "Ventriloquists are . . ." He thought for a moment. "Annoying," he said and winced. "And nobody really likes them."

Cathy brooded, arms folded, on the sofa. "That's not true," she said in a small voice. "A lot of people like them."

"Well, sure, a few morons in the audience chuckle," he went on, "but only because they're embarrassed for the ventriloquist. It's old hat. Fifties Vegas crap. That kind of humor doesn't appeal to us anymore." He hooked his thumbs into the belt loops of his jeans. "And I'm only talking about the traditional stuff. What you're attempting here—well, believe me,

Cathy. Nobody will have any patience for some poor confused little kid with a burnt log for a freakin' dummy."

"I like them," Cathy said, her braces glittering. "I do. Ventriloquists make me happy." She squeezed Marilyn tighter. "And I'm gonna be a world famous ventriloquist someday, whether you like it or not."

"Honey," he moaned, "it's burnt wood." He chopped the blade of his hand through the air. "Your dummy doesn't even have a mouth. Am I the only one in this house who sees that?" He turned to me. "Emmett, could you back me up here?"

"Dummies," I said to nobody in particular. "Dummies, dummies, dummies."

My father stared at me for a few seconds without speaking.

"Mom would let me do it," Cathy said to him. "Mom would *encourage* me."

My father twirled the lollipop stick in his mouth, ruminating. "I just don't get the attraction of ventriloquism. Really. I'm at a loss here. There are so many better options in the performing arts. That's all I'm saying." He shoved both hands in the back pockets of his jeans. "You know what the cool kids in school do? They sing and dance. It never goes out of style. What will the cool kids be doing a hundred years from now?"

"Singing and maybe dancing?" I said, casting a glance at Cathy, hoping she'd laugh with me.

"That's right, kiddo. You can't hold them back. Don't even try."

"I won't," I said.

Confident now of my accord, he turned his attention back to my sister. "But okay, if you insist on doing this, honey, I'll buy you a real dummy at the clown shop or whatever and you can—"

"Stop it!" Gawky, crazy-legged, swinging her pointed elbows, Cathy ran out of the family room and stomped up the stairs, trailing a whiff of scorch behind her. We heard her bedroom door slam shut overhead.

"Well, she's got a flair for the dramatic, I'll give her that," he said to me. "But I'm worried about that girl. What's gotten into her?"

Still seated on the floor, I smiled at my father. Shrugging, I turned up my palms, as if to say, "Pubescent girls: a mystery to us all." I felt pretty good about how things had turned out in our family. At one time I was the biggest troublemaker around. I was a source of constant concern. My parents' fear for my future was the mortar that held the bricks of our family together. Now, Mom was staying at Aunt Connie's house in Florida, trying not to snort cocaine with bikers. Cathy had fetishized a piece of firewood. My father was veering closer to his next alcoholic relapse. I was sitting pretty for once.

Dad stroked his goatee, that gingery eruption of hair on his face, and gazed out the family room window at our snow-plowed suburban street. Cathy's strange behavior had called into question so much that he had taken for granted, including his own hipness. He was forty-one years old, a marketing director for a local theater, a job that allowed him to dress and act like an artist—ponytail, earrings, jeans—yet still collect a businessman's steady paycheck. He liked avant-garde theater, but he was not cool enough to deal with the grotesque in his own home. He bit into the lollipop. Flakes of green candy clung to the inverted triangle of hair beneath his lower lip. He would have welcomed my mother's input in a situation like this. He looked down at me and frowned. "And what do you find so damned amusing, mister?"

Simple. Nobody was yelling at me. Cathy was a straight-A student and I was not. She played her clarinet with a dramatic flair that charmed adults and music teachers, and I couldn't even whistle. She had won awards for academic excellence, and I was often stuck in detention, which in my school was called JUG: Justice Under God. I was forced to write "conduct" and "discipline" repeatedly, in neat columns on lined paper, until my right hand went dead. Father Timothy sat at his desk scowling at us. He didn't even read a magazine or the newspaper. And if you said a single word to your neighbor, Father made you stand in the locked coat closet. You were in big trouble, kid, if he followed you in. So I was actually elated to see Cathy challenged by the same type of patriarchal oppression that I had grown so accustomed to and had been forced to counteract with an elaborate system of snorts, guffaws, and, on occasion, feigned loss of hearing.

Like most children, I spent up to twelve hours a day studying the erratic behavior of adults. Recognizing Dad's discomfort, I changed tactics. I wasn't quite sure if he had noted that, for once, we were on the same side. In my sweetest model-son voice, I said: "Cathy is behaving very badly, isn't she, Father?" I motioned with my crooked forefinger, so that he might bend down closer for a secret boy-to-man chat. "Maybe a little physical discipline might not be out of place. A belt whip across the calves?"

"Stop it, Emmett. That's terrible. Where do you come up with these things?" He kicked my dog's chew toy under the dining room table. Then he hitched up his sagging jeans and squatted before me like an aging baseball catcher. "Does she seem a little . . . "

"Spanking?" I said. "Good old spanking."

"All right, cut it out. You're not helping matters."

"Cathy's in trouble here," I reminded him, "not me."

"This is serious. Does she ever talk to you about her school or her friends there? What's the word on the street?"

Cathy went to Roosevelt Middle School, a four-story moron factory that warehoused close to two thousand kids from our zip code. Roosevelt produced a staggering population of head-bangers, gasoline-sniffers, Dungeons and Dragons freaks, sex addicts, arsonists-in-training and other future felons, and Dad thought that I might be prone to temptation there. I needed extra attention. The previous summer he'd found caffeine pills in my sock drawer. It concerned him. Pills at eleven meant LSD and heroin by sixteen. So he sent me to a private school, a Jesuit institution known for its moral rigidity, a place where vigilante priests patrolled the corridors eyeballing every backpack and lunchbox with the native distrust of border guards. One in par-ticular, Father Joe, would back me up against the lockers and ask an inane question just so he could peer into my eyeballs to see if my pupils were dilated. To this day, I don't know if he recognized in me a future stoner and was trying to prevent this terrible fate, or if all his excited talk about illicit substances and "what they could do to a boy" actually drove me to the bong by the age of fourteen.

"She's your sister, Emmett," my father said. "Aren't you concerned?"

"Don't yell at me. I hardly ever see her anymore." It was true. She walked to school with her girlfriends from the neigh-borhood, and I woke up an hour earlier to catch a bus to another zip code. It was dark as midnight each morning when I mounted the steps of the yellow bus.

My father leaned closer. "Hey," he said. "I'm not yelling at you. Okay, pal?" He squeezed my collarbone. I smelled the sour apple of his lollipop. "But I want you to stop talking like that. Cathy is your sister. You don't really want me to hurt her, do you?"

"Physical discipline," I said, low.

"Christ!" He turned away from me and walked out of the room. In the kitchen a cupboard door banged shut. "God, grant me the serenity," he recited. A moment later my father returned, his cheek bulging with fresh lollipop. "Let's have us a little chat, man to man. Now, I know you two kids think of yourselves as a team, but actually we're all on the same team, right? So give me the inside scoop, champ. Is your sister still super popular in the neighborhood?"

"She has lots of friends," I said, and then corrected myself. "She used to."

He nodded. "Minor setback. She'll win them back. So, in your opinion, who are the most popular kids nowadays? The singers, the dancers? Or the jocks?"

I shrugged.

"The nerds?" He smirked. "Have the nerds finally risen to the top?"

"Every cool kid is different, Dad."

"Right, right. It's the age of specialization. She's taking a big risk with this log thing, but who knows? It might pay off. You think it could?"

I was the wrong person to ask. My inability to keep up with the latest trends always unnerved him. The public and private schools, in his opinion, were a hotbed of ingenuity, a testing ground where a tribe of potential superstars sparred over the future of our culture's rites and rituals. I was too distracted to worry about any of that. After my mother moved to Florida without warning, I became the unofficial archivist of her debris. I inventoried the baubles on her bedside table. I straightened the photo I'd pinned on the fridge beneath a pineapple magnet. Nights, in my bedroom, I read her left-behind books, especially the photocopied working scripts from the roles she'd played at the theater. I fixated on her tiny pencil-scrawled notes in the margins: "Build." "Energy, energy, energy." "Brokenhearted."

"So what's your persona at school?" my father asked.

"My what?"

"You know, your identity, your vibe. What sets you apart from the pack?"

"Nothing," I said.

"That's loser talk, Emmett. Hey, you got any singers or dancers in that Jesuit school of yours? I bet you could make a big impact in that area."

He tucked the gummy lollipop stick behind his ear, one of the oddest moves I'd ever seen him make. That hapless white stick balanced over my father's ear like an unsmoked cigarette, giving him the look of a street tough in an old Hollywood movie, a ne'er-do-well loitering outside the pool hall. He cracked his knuckles and rose unsteadily to his feet. "Let me show you some moves. You'll be a hit at the next mixer."

"I'm gonna check on Cathy," I said, getting up from the floor.

"Okay! Now you're talking," he called after me. "Good man. Report back to me afterwards and we'll compare notes."

I climbed the stairs and knocked on Cathy's closed bedroom door. "Get lost, Emmett," she said.

I opened the door and stepped in. The bonfire aroma blended with all the other exotic smells of her bedroom: damp towels and washcloths; nail polish remover; sticky bottles of cheap perfume spot-welded to the dresser; cherry and grape lip gloss. Chest down on her bed, her ankles crossed in the air behind her, Cathy was flicking through the pages of a *Seventeen* magazine. The charred log, Marilyn, was reclining (prone? supine?) on the once-white pillowcase, just under Cathy's swaying feet. In the virginal setting of her bedroom, this black log was as conspicuous and disconcerting as an outpatient standing naked in traffic.

I sat down on the smudged pink comforter and placed my hand on her back, the way Dad sometimes did with me when I had a nightmare.

"I have gum in my room," I said, trying not to brag. "Hubba Bubba and Bubble Yum. I'll give you a piece. What's your favorite flavor?"

She ignored me.

"I might have Juicy Fruit, but I'd have to check first."

"I don't want any *gum*. God."

We sat in silence for half a minute, my sister smothering her tears while I searched for the right words.

"Want me to try to paint your toenails again?" I asked at last. "I can do it better this time."

"Just leave me alone, Emmett. Can't I ever have any privacy in this house?"

"I wish. Tell me about it," I said, employing two of her favorite expressions back-to-back to ingratiate myself with her. And for about three seconds, I gawked at the oily burnt stains on her pillowcases, knowing, even then, that they would never be clean again. "Hey, Cathy, you're right," I said. "Ventriloquists are cool."

She swung her face toward me. "Really? You think so?"

"Definitely."

"I've been practicing every night. I'm getting better, too. I think I'm actually pretty good."

"Well, that's what it takes. To get good, I mean."

"Do you want to see me do a routine?"

I told her I did, and honestly, I did. Even though my sister's sweat smelled foreign to me now and red blotches had surfaced on her chin, I still considered her my best friend. We hadn't spent much time together since Mom had left the house. Cathy's bedroom had become off limits. No boys allowed. So I felt honored by her invitation to watch a private performance.

She propped the burnt log on her lap. Ashy fingerprint swirls adorned her pale forehead. Her smudged yellow T-shirt called to mind a demented crossbreed of Charlie Brown and Pigpen. "Okay," she said. "Here goes." She took a deep breath and shouted, "It's a nice day today, isn't it, Marilyn?" She bounced her left knee once, hard, and ashes fell to the rug.

"Mmm-hmm!" Marilyn said.

Cathy looked down at Marilyn as though she were a newborn baby. "Do you like going to school, Marilyn?" she asked in a loud voice.

"Mmm-hmm!" Marilyn said.

"That's good." Cathy laughed. "School is important. But it's also really tough for a lot of people. Will you be ready for seventh grade, you think?"

Marilyn thought about it for a moment, considered the possibilities before answering definitively: "Mmm-hmm!"

My sister stared at me with raised eyebrows. "So? What do you think?" A loose strand of blond hair fell over her eyes. She pushed her lower lip out and blew the curl back.

"Wow," I said.

"Mrs. Palermo says I have a 'unique talent.' Remember when I told you about Mister Charleston and Woody coming for assembly? They were really great and everybody loved it when Mr. Charleston drank that orange juice and Woody sang 'Feelings.' Whoa oh oh feelings." My sister searched my eyes for an answer. "Isn't that cool?"

Cathy had been damaged. I understood that I, too, would soon be transformed. The mystical word "puberty" blazed in my head.

"Well, if Mom's not back soon," Cathy said, "I'm going to Florida to live with her. She'll let me do what I want." Cathy motioned to her oppressor downstairs. "I mean, if I love it, shouldn't that be what matters? Why can't he understand that? Why won't he let me?"

I patted her forearm. "Because all grownups are dick-heads?"

Cathy smiled at me. I smiled back. We burst out laughing.

At that moment, we were as close as we had been since Mom left for Florida.

It didn't last.

"Hey Cath," I said, regaining my breath. "I know how we can use Marilyn for something really great."

"How?" she said uncertainly. A vertical crease appeared between her eyes.

"Well, what Dad needs, I think, is a little physical discipline." I nodded my head at this inevitable conclusion. "He's being very bad, isn't he? So maybe you could bake a chocolate cake and we'll crush the stupid log inside it. He'll eat the cake and then he'll flop around on the kitchen floor, choking, and we can cram his nostrils full of peanuts while he cries."

"What?" Cathy blinked at me. "I'm not gonna feed Marilyn to Dad. What are you, a maniac? It would kill him."

"Well, maybe we should tie him to the tree out back and pour honey and Kool-Aid all over him, and then break an ant farm on his head." I laughed and reached for Marilyn.

Cathy jumped up. "What are you talking about, Emmett? He's our father. Are you joking, or what?"

"Just forget it." I glared at the double rainbow poster on her wall. "I was only kidding."

Regrettably, in that instant, I saw that nothing had changed between us. Oh, Cathy could dabble in darkness, but when foolish, spontaneous, and possibly fatal decisions were required, my sister invariably turned her back and went skipping toward the light. She would eventually go to high school and become involved with music clubs, Track and Field, and animal rights organizations. She'd earn high grades and head off to a university in Boston. Her days as an innovative ventriloquist would be long forgotten.

In my eyes she was a lost cause. A training bra dangled over the back of her desk chair. She couldn't pass a mirror without checking her teeth and hair and inspecting her profile. Something secret and horrible was going on in her bedroom at night, something that didn't include me.

That night I left her bedroom with hardly a backward glance. I trotted down the carpeted stairs, kicked open the back door and hopped down the slushy cement steps. Snow crunched underneath my sneakers in the driveway.

Bones was galloping around the backyard, his ears flapping. I noticed that he'd knocked over his water dish and had chewed up one of Dad's winter gloves. "Up to a little mischief again, are you, boy?" I shook my finger at him. His wet brown eyes flashed at the sight of me. "Maybe you need somebody to teach you some manners." Bones started panting and hopping around as I neared him. "Follow orders! Pay attention!" I said. "Get in the coat closet! Listen to Father Timothy!" I grabbed Bones' collar and yanked him closer to me. "What you need, I think, is a little physical discipline. Then you'll know how to behave."

But Bones, he didn't understand. He was just a puppy.

MEN'S ROOM

We are dancing to Shostakovich in a Taco Bell men's room in Utica, New York.

Grabowski says, "I got a cache full of fire words and scads of time, rooster." The acoustics of the men's room are top notch, and our man Shosty has never sounded more robust, but there's room for only two men in here at any given time. Tonight we are four and feeling the pinch. No one disagrees with Grabowski but Leach is laughing hard, too hard, in my opinion, and he's making everyone feel unsafe.

Leach's bio: love-avoidant GED recipient, always picks Ratt's "Round and Round" on Karaoke Nite, uses the term "comeuppance" with alarming frequency. I feel his hot breath on my earlobe. I can't escape the reach of his breath. We are too constricted here and he knows this, Leach does, and he uses it to his filthy advantage. "Grabowski ain't got the gumption to glimmer newfangle," he says in my ear. "You gonna need fibrocon consolation jacks to fortify that foundation, posthaste."

Cleaver's been taking an origami night class at the community center. I'm watching him transform a wad of toilet paper into an African elephant. His hands are a blur, his tongue-tip clenched between his teeth. When he finishes, he grins and says, "Voilà."

Door opens behind me, bangs into my back. A smirker in a bloodred Che T forces his way into our sanctuary. He wedges his body between Grabowski and Cleaver to get at the urinal. Now we are five and completely immobilized. And just when we thought it couldn't get any warmer in here, another man—bearded, insolent, with sharp elbows—fights his way to the mirror, where he inspects the contours of his bristly face. He spits on his fingertip and runs his finger along the length of each eyebrow. Evidently they are 'brows that require not a little saliva to hold in place. Then he works a wooden toothpick between his lower teeth. I cannot look away.

"Dance party?" Grabowski says.

Me (shrugging): "Why not?"

Cleaver: "Spank the torque out of my dingus maker. I'm fixing to canoodle with death."

Eyebrows: "The fuck?"

Che: "Patria o Muerte!"

Leach, as always, colonizes the final word: "Stick dog wears a yellow beak and I'm fat fat fat. Hop to it, boys. The water's fine."

We start moving again and snapping our fingers. Cleaver ejects the Shostakovich cassette and inserts a Sibelius symphony, darker music with haunting modal implications, and Leach shoves the 'brow groomer into Che Guevara who uncorks a spray of fantastic profanity and Grabowski throws a left uppercut, misses, and the boomboombox slips off the sink and smashes on the dirty tile floor and Leach lets fly with a wild right hook that catches me in the mouth and the lights go out and when they come back on I am on the floor and Grabowski is standing on my abdomen. "Grabowski!" I say.

Cleaver has a tambourine.

THE LIFE SHE'S
BEEN MISSING

Nine people exit the movie theater: four couples and Addie. She stands under the dripping marquee and shakes open her cheap umbrella, a move that attracts the attention of a man loitering by his Lexus. He plucks the red plastic coffee stirrer from his mouth and tucks it in his breast pocket. A weird gesture, she thinks, a bit gross, but kind of endearing.

"Your umbrella's shot," he calls out.

Addie nods and looks down at her cell phone. No missed messages. It's definitely on, but nobody has called.

Dimitri is probably having sex right now with one of the waitresses at the bar, most likely the blonde from Jersey City with the pretty singing voice and the easy laugh.

"How'd you like the movie?" the man asks, approaching her.

This one has a matador's face, she thinks, insolent and beautiful. "It was okay," she says. "Kind of shallow and derivative, but I didn't really expect much going into it."

Derivative. That should scare him.

"Agreed," he says. "That flick was bullshit." He arches his neck and lampoons the American actors' failed British accents—"Blewdy hell, it's pissin'!"—and in spite of herself, Addie laughs.

His name is Rob, he says. And hers?

Four minutes later, he's strolling back to his Lexus with her number in his cell phone.

Back at her apartment, Addie keeps checking her phone. No missed messages. To take her mind off Dimitri and the blonde, she flips open her laptop and scrolls through responses to her online-dating profile.

Suitor 11: "Why you don't smile in you photos? You think your better than everybody?"

Suitor 14: "How do you want it???"

Suitor 19: "Can I ask you a question. Under the heading 'The most private thing I'm willing to admit,' I see that you've written 'snitches get stitches.' Care to elaborate?"

Suitor 20: "suck wang"

Suitor 22: "Greetings. My name is Martin Josovich. I am a retired History teacher. I am seventy-three years old, but I'm blessed with more *joie de vivre* and enthusiasm than men half my age. My dear Sadie, may she rest in peace, could testify to this. Were she watching me, and I believe she is, she'd be saying, 'Get out there, Marty. Meet someone new.' Help me make her wishes come true."

Addie sighs and closes her laptop and wonders if she made a mistake by giving Rob her number. He is, after all, a complete stranger. He could be violent or boring. He probably won't even call. Of course he won't call.

Rob calls on the third night. Normally when she's on the phone, Addie paces around the apartment and thumbs through books while the other person talks; or she scrolls through Netflix for new releases; or she eats raspberries from the carton with the fridge door open. But Rob has a pleasant voice and a great sense of humor that makes her want to do none of these things. A few times she laughs out loud, a good sign.

That night in the shower Addie replays the entire twelve-minute conversation. Rob wants to pick her up at noon on Saturday. Another good sign. Some guys can wring only an Italian dinner and a Hollywood-movie-plus-drinks out of their repertoires and can't imagine picking up a woman before dark. This date will be different.

Before going to sleep, Addie boils a pot of dandelion tea and works on her manuscript for an hour. When her eyes get too tired, she tosses the pages on the mantel, takes off her glasses, and turns off most of the lights in the apartment. On some nights, like this one, she can't stop replaying the voice of her college boyfriend. "You're so romantically immature, Addie." With their backs to the wall they sat naked, not touching, on his mattress on the floor. "You're far too pretty and smart to be this insecure. Why can't you just be cool?" In the kitchen Addie sticks a bundle of fresh lavender in a jar, which she puts on the table beside her bed.

Why can't you just be cool?

On Saturday at precisely noon Rob's black Lexus pulls up in front of Addie's building. She notices the vanity plates: I DOCTOR. Does this mean he's an optometrist? An ophthalmologist? What's the difference again? She won't even bring it up, she decides. She'll compliment his car or his hair instead. She will be very cool.

Addie slides into the passenger seat and smiles at Rob. "You look great," he says—this from a man who has made clear vision his vocation—and merges expertly into traffic.

The city rolls by her window, and she is relieved to find that Rob doesn't feel a need to talk much. The music is too loud, for one thing, and the stereo speakers are everywhere, above, below, side to side, playing a maniacally cheerful pop song.

Rob guns the engine on the FDR North and taps his thumbs on the steering wheel.

"Glad it's Saturday," he says at last.

She smiles at him. "Me, too."

He presses a button on the steering wheel, activating a third repeat of the same song. "Totally," he says, before lapsing again into silence.

What a pleasant change from Dimitri, who would never stop talking. She met him in the kitchen of a house party in Brooklyn. Addie waited with an empty cup while a guy in a muscle shirt pumped the keg and droned on about a Bolaño novel to a lanky redhead with tattoos on his forearms. Dimitri appeared beside Addie, frowned at the redhead, who was now expertly tilting his cup at a foam-reducing angle, and said, "Greased lightning over here, eh?" She didn't know why it was funny, but it was. She laughed.

"This young lady is practically dehydrated, fellas," Dimitri said to them. "Stop mucking about."

When they finished, Dimitri took the keg nozzle and filled her cup first, then his own. She wasn't looking for old-fashioned manners in a man, but, she told her girlfriends, from that very first night, Dimitri *saw* her, understood her.

Rob pulls the car into a mall parking lot. Addie looks out the window and realizes she doesn't know where they are. Queens? Long Island?

Rob swings open his door. "Let's hit it," he says.

"The mall?" Still strapped to the seat, she forces a smile. "Really?"

"This place cracks me up," he says. "Come on."

In the video arcade, Rob slips a five-dollar bill into a change machine, and she watches twenty tokens blast into the brass bowl below. Grinning, he hands Addie eight tokens and swings his arm out as if introducing her to a magical realm. "Play whatever you want. It's on me."

She's met well-off men before, and they're invariably different from what you first expect. They do things that nobody would imagine a person of their stature doing. Rob, she notices, doesn't need to dress in an Armani suit to attract attention to his wealth. He wears a ragged tweed sport coat over a Bruce Lee T-shirt. His dark wash jeans and black Chuck Taylors complete the look he seems to be going for. And this unorthodox beginning to their date doesn't entirely repel her. On the contrary, it strangely comforts her, because she will not have to put on an act with this guy. She can be herself with Rob. It's too much pressure these days to date an indie-rock drummer or a coke-snorting sculptor, the guys who want to go to after-hours parties and talk about the great artistic work they're not doing. They always deem her too conservative, too tame, and end up leaving for a bony woman with bangs and a spider tattoo on her thigh.

She stands beside Rob at a kung fu video game—her legs and arms goose-fleshed from the air-conditioning—and realizes that she's even more attracted to him than she had first thought. Tongue tip peeking through clenched lips, dark eyebrows crunched down over his nose—he is undeniably handsome. There really are some good men out there, she decides. Kindhearted, charming sweethearts. She knew it all along. She just needed to look harder. Here's a fun-loving, generous guy with a positive demeanor, the opposite of Dimitri, that self-destructive moper, whose harrowing descents into despair were numbed only by copious amounts of vodka, ice cream, and kettle corn. Like some kind of computer-animation trick, Dimitri morphed into a fat, alcoholic bartender when she wasn't looking. One moment he was a beautiful boy at a party, making flirty jokes with her, and the next thing she knew, *wham*. Old Fat Beard.

She's lucky Dimitri dumped her, though it shattered her at the time. *He* broke up with *her*: she hadn't seen that coming. But it wasn't a breakup so much as an act of liberation. In fact, she should send him a thank-you note.

Rob shouts, "Press the KICK button for me! Be on my side."

She's ecstatic. She pushes that KICK button for all she's worth. On the game screen two cartoonishly muscular villains fall and die, thanks to her help.

Rob breaks free from the game long enough to plant a wet kiss on her cheek. Before Addie can even react, he's banging away at the PUNCH button with the heel of his hand. "Fuck," he says and snaps his fingers. "Check it out," he says, pointing to the screen. "I got killed by that priest guy and his special powers. Wait, I'm getting back up. I'm still alive! Am I? No, I'm not getting back up. Yup. I'm dead."

She puts her hand on his back and rubs between his shoulder blades, and helps him through this minor emotional crisis—their first as a couple—and he smiles gratefully at her. "Strange as it sounds," she imagines telling someone, "we were in an arcade when I just knew."

He motions to Sbarro and says, "You hungry? Let's grab a slice."

"Sure, but do you really want to stay here?"

He looks puzzled by her question, his eyebrows converging. "Why not?"

"You're right," she says, laughing. "Why not?"

"I'm having fun," he says.

"I'm having a blast," she says, her voice a little too enthusiastic. She reaches out and touches his forearm. "I love pizza. Well, okay, I don't *love* it. It's not my favorite food in the world, but it's up there. Is it your favorite?"

"Nope," he says.

And that's it. Nothing more. Guys can do that. *Nope.* Easy as that.

Addie and Rob stare into each other's eyes, and a gulf of silence opens between them. She realizes she hasn't said anything remotely interesting or smart since he picked her up. Look at that glum face, she thinks. It's obvious what he's thinking right now. He's worried that he's made a mistake and picked a dim woman.

"Hey." He leans closer, his nose scrunched. "I think somebody farted. Do you smell it? Damn, that's ripe. Let's get out of here."

Addie leans back in the booth, sated after a slice of mushroom pizza and a quart of orange soda. She realizes that *this* is the life she's been missing. Simple, unadorned pleasure. Who needs fine dining with its confusion of utensils, plates, and stemware? Who needs entry into exclusive clubs where only the holiest are permitted to worship? Shared time at the mall, doing nothing, just being together with your man—that's what's important. Dimitri, wearing only unwashed gym shorts, spent hours watching the Yankees on his enormous TV or napping on the couch before his nightly shifts at the bar, and she felt ridiculous as she hopped around him on Saturday afternoons, saying, "Want to go to the park? There's jazz in the park, Dimitri. Want to fly a kite? Go out to lunch? Anything you want, because today's your day, killer."

But Dimitri only smacked his lips and yawned and drifted off to sleep on the couch. That wasn't shared time. That wasn't the mall arcade in Queens. (Or Long Island?) Rob isn't like Dimitri at all. Rob is a doer. And that was probably the biggest problem she had with Old Fat Beard toward the end. She was making all the decisions, and it's thrilling to be with someone who says, Today *I'm* making the decisions. I'm taking *you* out. You don't have to worry about a thing. You're in my capable hands.

Rob licks pizza grease from his fingers and tells her that his "pants are vibrating." He fishes out his smartphone, an expensive-looking device that can probably make waffles from scratch. He glances at the caller, blushes, and excuses himself. "Sorry. Have to take this. I'll be white black."

Addie laughs—she always laughs when she's uncomfortable, a tic she dislikes about herself—and wonders whose call is significant enough to get him away from the table. Another woman? Girlfriend? Wife? Why did she ever think that this man was single? Of course he's married. Or engaged, at least. His tall, classy fiancée is probably some fashion model from Copenhagen who would never set foot in the mall. *That's* why Rob brought her here. Cruel and clever. But what does that Danish beauty have that Addie doesn't, other than two passports and towering height? Maybe Addie can win Rob away from her. No, she shouldn't break up a potential marriage.

It was good while it lasted, she thinks. This date got you out of your apartment, and you're finally seeing Queens or Long

Island through the food-court window. Another guy will come along soon.

Unless he doesn't. And the truth is none will if she's too passive. So why give one up when he's already here?

Addie watches Rob pace outside Sbarro with his greasy fingers pressing the phone to his ear. Clearly Rob needs an attentive woman. He can't take care of himself properly. He needs comfort and nurturing and disinfecting wipes for his sticky hands. But that's not her job. Best to end this thing before she gets too deep.

Addie drapes her cardigan over her shoulders like a shawl and walks toward Rob, prepared to tell him that she's taking a taxi home. Maybe he'll protest and drive her back to Manhattan, and maybe they'll make out for a while in front of her building, but that's it. He may kiss her, but he's not coming up. Well, he can come up for one cup of coffee, but the bra is not—not!—coming off. Sorry, Rob. And even if it does become unhooked somehow, even if it falls to the floor by mistake or divine intervention, no way are they crossing the threshold to her bedroom. Two condoms are hidden in her bedside drawer, in case of an emergency. Unprotected sex is not even an option. Rob will have to wear a condom. That's non-negotiable.

"Rob?" she says, her voice barely a whisper.

"Why?" he says into the phone, unaware of her. "You told me I could keep it until dinnertime. Yes, you did. You *did*. Fine. I'll bring it back in an hour. Please?" His voice climbs a register as he says, "Dad, *please*. I'll finish my homework later. I'm on a date with a *girl*."

Addie backs away from Rob into a sporting-goods store, where she hides behind a display of dangling baseball mitts to collect her thoughts. She glances at her watch: 4:18 p.m. A steady progression of days, months, years has dragged her to this very spot. She's twenty-six years old and evidently on a mall date with a high-school kid. Utterly humiliating. But how could she have known? After all, Rob does look like he's in his mid-twenties. And, in her defense, she still looks "fresh" and "tight" at twenty-six, if the opinion of InsaneSexxxClown666 (Suitor 30) counts for anything. In grocery stores and bodegas she still has to show her ID to purchase alcohol. So this is all easily explainable.

A man in a green polo shirt steps around the display of baseball mitts. His nametag reads WADE. "Help you find something?"

My God, she can't escape them. They are everywhere, men and boys, these prowling animals with their hairy faces and big hands. "No, thank you," she says. "Just looking."

"The Mizuno is a great glove." He grabs a black mitt from the wall, plunges his hand inside it, and punches his fist into the leather. "Big pocket. Good action. Want to try it?"

"I have to go," she says. "Thanks."

"Any time," he calls out. "Come back, ask for Wade, and I'll take care of you."

She exits the mall through the store's side door, her face burning. She wants to view this as a wake-up call, a chance to make some positive changes in her life. She should call Rob later tonight and thank him. No, he should never know the truth. Let it be a mystery. Besides, he has homework to finish.

There are no taxis in the parking lot. She can't see a bus stop anywhere. Just sit for a minute, she tells herself. Breathe.

Sit right here on this bench and don't look at your phone. Yes. That's good. Shut your eyes. Relax. Feel the wind on your face.

A month later, Addie revises her online-dating profile, answering every question honestly, no lies at all, and giving a straightforward appraisal of her life and what she's looking for in a partner. Four weeks removed from the Rob debacle, she recognizes the importance of complete honesty from the get-go. She provides her real age and favorite movies and TV shows and reveals her true personality, not some imagined ideal that she thinks will appeal to someone brilliant and successful. Dozens of men in the tri-state area contact her.

Suitor 237: "Have you tried the dating scene and found it lacking? Me, too. So let's save each other from any more awkward situations. Meet me at the YMCA swimming pool. Wear that little two piece [wink-wink], and we'll just see what we're made of. Afterward maybe we'll smoke some hash. I'm sober, but AA doesn't say jack about drugs. Let's get together."

Suitor 245: "BIG! Trust me."

Suitor 251: "I read your profile with no small amount of interest. You seem kind. In case you're wondering about my photos, yes, that is an authentic Austrian woodsman's hat from the Kingdom of Bavaria. Bet you've never seen a hat like that before. Have you?"

Ultimately, Addie chooses to reply to Suitor 263 in Brooklyn, who wrote: "Hey. You're pretty. Wanna meet for coffee?"

"Sure," she writes. "Can you come to Manhattan?"

He doesn't write back.

At work on a Monday in early March, when winter is still at war with spring, Addie takes a break from data entry and opens an issue of *Us Weekly*. Dimitri once said, "Why do you always gotta read that rag? It's trash." And she told him it was the same to her as watching professional baseball or soccer was to him: a diversion. "But the difference is," he said, "I don't imagine I'm one of the players. You act like you know them, Addie. It's messing with your mind." It was the wrong thing to say, however truthful. She stood up and walked out of the room, slamming the door behind her. "Why don't you update your blog," he shouted, "or write another chapter of that novel you're supposedly working on?"

After a few minutes' thought, she puts down the magazine and approaches the office of Marge Pistorek, her boss, who has always intimidated Addie. Perhaps it's the way she barrels through the office, a plump cannonball ready to smash into anything, looking over shoulders to see what's on people's screens.

Marge looks up from the papers on her desk and says, "What's up?"

"Hi. I'm really sorry, but I think I might want to leave."

"Leave where?"

Addie coughs. "The job. My job." She coughs again. "I'm considering moving on."

Her boss sighs. "Fine. But you're staying two more weeks, right?"

"I guess I'm more, like, looking for advice."

"Two weeks is standard."

"Do you think I should stay? Am I doing a good job? No, what I'm really wondering is: is there a way for me to do more creative work for the company? I'm an ambitious, thoughtful—"

"Tell you what: stay another week. In fact, I can probably replace you by this Thursday, Friday at the latest. Can you stay three days? Can you give me that?"

"Yes," Addie says. "I mean, no, I can stay the full two weeks. You know, I don't even have to leave."

"Not necessary. Two, three days, tops. Thanks for letting me know."

At Brown University, Addie had a close friend, Robin, who, like Addie, had lost her mother at an early age. As juniors Addie and Robin became the youngest co-editors in the history of *The Round*, the undergraduate literary magazine. They often stayed up drinking red wine in Slater Hall. In Robin's dorm room they smoked weed and blew the smoke through a toilet-paper roll stuffed with fabric-softener sheets to hide the smell. Then they ordered Peking duck from the place around the corner. They liked trudging stoned through the snow in their parkas and boots, talking about the latest submissions, vowing to publish more women writers, more writers of color, more innovative stuff. The food was always cold by the time they returned, but it didn't matter at all. Addie spent three nights in Robin's narrow dorm bed. Afterward, when it became clear that they were compatible only as platonic friends, neither spoke of it again.

This rupture wounded Addie more than she ever admitted, especially when Robin began dating Ava, a talented visual artist who lived off campus. Addie's co-editor and best friend couldn't find time for her anymore. It had only been a fling, she told herself then, a failed experiment.

At Martini Navratilova, the hole-in-the-wall bar on Avenue B, she drinks oily red wine at eight dollars a glass. Within minutes of her arrival, she falls into a conversation with an attractive gray-haired woman in her early fifties. When it's time for a refill, the woman, Susan, ignores Addie's request for red wine and buys her a "real drink": a Jack Daniel's, neat.

"I wouldn't touch the wine they serve here," Susan says. "I don't know what's in it exactly, but it ain't grapes."

Addie learns that Susan edits a popular series of chick-lit novels. Susan lets out a derisive laugh when speaking about it. Pink and lime-green covers, a lot of bad writing inside. Susan says she has toyed with the idea of calling the series *For Masochists Only*.

Addie had read one of the books at the Hamptons house her friends rented a few summers ago. She'd found it on a living-room shelf, a single spine-cracked volume amidst miscellaneous tchotchkes. The truth is, she'd enjoyed how light it was, perfect for skimming while sipping wine under an oak tree.

"Actually I read one of your books," Addie says. "I liked it."

"They're garbage." Susan assesses Addie over the rim of her glass with her pretty, narrowed eyes. "They're cotton candy."

"But sometimes you're in the mood for that."

"If you have no taste."

Addie coughs. "Then why do you edit them?"

"Oh, I don't know. A little thing called a mortgage?"

"But you seem so intelligent. Couldn't you—"

She raises her hand to stop Addie. "You're cute but annoying. Have a good night."

"Who is this?" Old Fat Beard says in a low voice, almost whispering into the phone.

"It's me," she says. "I'm drunk and just left a lesbian bar and everything is shit."

"Mom?" he asks.

Addie hangs up, horrified, but then calls him right back. "Dimitri?"

"That was a joke," he says.

She lets out a tired laugh. She does not yet know the thirty-six-year-old Addie who will become managing editor of *Nylon* magazine, the forty-four-year-old first-time novelist, the sixty-two-year-old breast-cancer survivor. These future versions of herself are as hard to reconcile with who she is today—a drunk young woman on the corner of 7th and B, her phone pressed to her ear—as the five-year-old child who fell down the stairs and sobbed into her mother's papery neck, the angry eleven-year-old who refused to speak at her mother's funeral, the fourteen-year-old who won a writing award for a short story about a dying pet but didn't bother to show up at the after-school ceremony to claim her prize.

"I've been thinking about you," Dimitri says.

Her legs are carrying her toward his apartment. "Good thoughts?"

"Hells yeah. You know I love you, Addie. Come over?"

"I don't know. I've been drinking, and it's late."

"Uh-huh." She can hear his enormous TV on low volume in the background. "Well, your contact-lens case and saline solution are still in the bathroom."

"Aw. That's sweet." Also quite strange, because it's been over six months since he broke up with her.

Dimitri coughs into the phone. "I have a cold. Just warning you in advance."

She doesn't care. They can be sick together, cuddled under a blanket. "I'm sick, too," she says, as if this confirms their compatibility. "I've been coughing all night."

She hears the TV's volume grow a little louder. "Would you mind bringing over a twelve-pack?" he says. "The fridge is kind of empty."

She stops on the corner. Her kitchen and her desk and her friends and her life are in the other direction. It's raining now. Freezing cold. Her ankles are soaked.

She knows she shouldn't go to him.

She knows that.

Please. Tell her something she doesn't know.

A DOMESTIC TYRANNY

The new puppy entered without knocking. He trotted right past us in the living room, his pink tongue flapping spit on the carpet. He was a stout white dog, about knee-high, with a brown blotch on his back. The kids were thrilled. "I love him," my son said. "A new puppy," my daughter said. "He's beautiful."

After my children and wife had gone to sleep, I slipped out of bed for a glass of water. Despite the lateness of the hour, the puppy's bedroom light was still on. I knocked, two light taps, then opened his door. "Everything okay in here?" I said in a friendly tone, peeking my head in the room. "How are you settling in? Need anything?"

The puppy was reaching his paw under the bed. Clearly he was concealing something under there, pushing it in deeper with his paw.

"What do you think you're doing?" I said.

The puppy spun around and barked with terrible ferocity. He lunged at me, his sharp teeth bared. Startled, I pulled the door shut and retreated down the hall.

The following morning, at breakfast, I called a family meeting. I wanted to nip this puppy situation in the bud. My wife Mary Ellen claimed that she had a stack of student papers to grade. She was already way behind on her work. "Not now, honey," she said. "I'm really really busy. Rain check?"

But I was adamant. Call me old-fashioned, but I still preferred the traditional way of choosing a dog. Once upon a time, you took your wife and kids to the kennel or the pound, and you shook hands with the candidates, rubbed their bellies, checked them for infirmities or open sores. You tried to imagine if this one or that one would be a good match for your family. But this brash new puppy circumvented this time-tested democratic system. By inviting himself into our home, he seemed to be setting a dangerous precedent. I considered it my duty to point this out to my family. We had to act swiftly. The children, I could see, were already smitten. The puppy reminded them of themselves: he was clumsy, playful, and indifferent to any rules that impeded mindless fun and instant gratification.

As a human resources manager, I had learned to confront possible misunderstandings head-on, ASAP, in a straightforward and adult fashion, bringing opposing parties to the negotiating table. I scheduled another family meeting for that same evening, an unprecedented "two-fer" that I hoped underscored the urgency of the situation.

I opened the meeting informally, ignoring the conventions of Robert's Rules. "I think you all know why we're here." Normally, of course, I would have followed the proper order of business, but I wanted to address the hot-button issue immediately. The puppy couldn't hear us, I hoped. Who knew what he was doing behind the closed door of his bedroom? Concealing bones beneath the bureau, I imagined. "We have a situation on our hands," I said. "It's this new puppy."

"Let's call him Tex," my son Charlie said. "Tex is a really good name for a dog. Brian has a new dog—and guess what his name is? Tex."

I shook my head. "No, I don't think so, son." I placed my palms flat on the table. "You see, naming a dog only breeds familiarity—"

"Tex, Tex," echoed Alice. She had a brown smear on her cheek that might have been dirt, might have been chocolate.

"All in favor?" asked Mary Ellen, her green pen lodged behind her right ear. Three hands raised. "Motion carries." She rose from the table, papers tucked under her arm, and left the room. "Meeting adjourned," she said over her shoulder. The kids hopped down from their chairs and ran into the kitchen, seeking popsicles and hours of puppy play.

Admiringly, I watched my wife return to her apple-shaped indentation on the sofa, where she would grade papers for the rest of the evening. Nobody said Mary Ellen wasn't efficient. She was a veritable Who's Who in our family, a woman who scored off the charts in the Expected Value Ratio and McKinsey's 7-S Framework. A tremendous motivational speaker, a thirty-four-year-old dynamo known for her quick wit and willingness to work overtime, Mary Ellen had made my list of Ones To Watch for the coming year. I had done my due diligence, held out for a full buy-in partner with more than just core competency, and was reaping the rewards.

Was I the only one who recognized the serious problem we had on our hands? Tex was not a team player. Tex was a negative cash flow drain that could not be justified in the year-end bookkeeping. I was confident that when my family reviewed the quarterly budget—copies of which I distributed to each of them, thumbtacking the printouts to the bulletin boards outside their bedrooms—they would agree that Tex was not contributing any tangible gain to the family's resources. Tex was a spoiled, erratic, lone-wolf type who couldn't be counted on at crunch time.

Willy, our previous dog, an ASPCA acquisition, used to leave his bedroom door open. You'd pass in the hallway and it was nice to see him in there working. "Hiya, Willy," you'd say chummily. Or, "Warm out tonight, eh, Willy?" It was comfortable. He was about as laid-back a pet as a family could hope for. Part yellow Lab, part mongrel, Willy spent hours licking his testicles, keeping everything polished and up to snuff.

This new puppy ignored me when I talked to him. He yawned until I was finished speaking, his long curling pink tongue jutting from his mouth. His entitled behavior suggested that *I* was the interloper in the house, not him. It unnerved me, but nobody else seemed to notice. That was the brilliance of his plan. He knew that the others would think that I had the problem, that I needed help. It was crafty, I grant the puppy that. Willy, for all his slobbery charm, was far less calculating.

After watching Tex act out all week long, ignoring every single law I had devised, making unilateral decisions about slipper destruction and invasion of bedrooms, I called another family meeting. Mary Ellen groaned, took off her glasses, and rubbed her eyes. "Not a chance," she said. "I've got thirty papers to grade."

But I was adamant. Everybody showed up.

Charlie and Alice climbed up onto the big-person chairs and awaited further instructions. I viewed them as reliable team members with excellent attendance numbers and high scores in the most valuable areas of family life: love, loyalty, and punctuality.

"Has anybody noticed anything . . . odd . . . about the puppy?" I began, after taking silent roll call with my eyes. "Anything? Go ahead and say the first thing that comes to your mind, even if it's negative."

"Tex fetched today," Charlie said. "He fetched in the backyard. I threw a stick in the air and he—"

"Okay, fine," I said. "Tex fetched a stick. Duly noted. What else? Alice?"

"I love Tex." Charlie laughed and smacked his sticky little hands down on the edge of the table. "Tex runs and jumps and can catch the stick."

"That's enough, son," I said, shaking my pencil at him. "You had your turn. Relinquish the floor, please."

Charlie was a hard-working six-year-old, a spunky right-brain thinker with leadership potential, a pacesetter with good instincts who sometimes, unfortunately, had a tendency to reach for the lowest hanging fruit. However, he was an opinionated little contributor who knew exactly what he wanted, though his heated emotions governed his behavior early in the morning and late at night. Helicopter view: you could count on Charlie in crunch time.

"Tex!" he said again.

Dammit, where was our loyalty to old Willy? Was this simply "how life goes," as they say, in the leafy sheltered confines of our neighborhood? Out with the old dog and in with the new? The old dog forgotten like last week's pop star—no bon voyage, no portrait above the mantel, nothing? And the new dog systematically deconstructing the previous dog's best work while we stood by and passively watched?

"Alice?" I said, touching my daughter's hand. "Has Tex bitten you? Has he been a very bad dog? Would you like to file a formal complaint against him?"

"Nuh uh," she said, shaking her head. "Tex fetched the stick."

Slight-of-build but refreshingly enthusiastic, prone to follow the pack with no inclination to lead, Alice was a supportive team player, a five-year-old with a good head on her shoulders and an ear for the telling detail. She had not yet impressed me with her intelligence or her work ethic, but one couldn't expect a great deal from such a new member of the team. She was still learning the ropes in terms of contributing. Root-and-branch view: Outstanding potential. Gradual improvement required.

Tex was trouble, a red flag poster boy. He got himself into the latticework, into the macaroni salad, into mud puddles. Tex nipped ankles, scratched, howled, whimpered. He squirted our cut pile carpet with his pungent urine. He downloaded pornography on the Internet—unless it was Charlie. Or Alice. Or Mary Ellen. Or me. And Tex was building something in his room, something dangerous. One night, late, I thought I heard him working with a drill or a lathe. The next morning I tried to get a look in there when Tex was out doing his aerobic exercises in the backyard, but every time I tried to peek my head into his room, Tex would bolt through the door flap and tear around the corner so fast, his ridiculous tongue flapping, that I had to pretend I was straightening a picture on the wall outside his door. He growled until I went away.

On a Monday morning in March, about two months after Tex moved into our home, I called in sick to work after yet another sleepless night. My nerves were simply too frazzled to be an effective workplace contributor. My supervisor Manny, a Latino go-getter, a successful left-brain thinker and a textbook ENTJ on the Myers-Briggs scale, suggested that I drink some Red Bull and get my "fat shitty ass in gear."

While I was on the phone, Tex urinated on the kitchen floor. Right in front of me! And then he stood there looking up at me, as if to say: "That happened. You gonna do anything about it?" What would I do about it? We both knew the answer. I'd get down on my hands and knees and clean it up. What choice did I have?

I told Manny I wouldn't be able to come in that day. "Things are heating up over here."

"Maybe you should heat your résumé up while you're at it," he said.

At night, in bed, Mary Ellen glared at me as if I were a stranger. I blamed Tex for this. He was ruining everything we held dear. How could we go on pretending he wasn't destroying our family? Mary Ellen told me to get a grip.

The kids avoided me. They had chosen sides. Clearly they loved this puppy and had forgotten Willy and all that he had accomplished in his eight years with us. That's when I understood that Willy had been my dog, my favorite, and Tex was theirs. I convened no more family meetings.

Sleep eluded me. In vivid and recurring nightmares I heard the click-click-click of Tex's claws on the linoleum floor, the sound growing progressively louder. Click-click-click. I sat bolt upright in bed, sweating and chilled. Mary Ellen pressed herself against the wall, moving away from me.

Morning in America. The smell of eggs and toast in the air. Coffee percolating, the radio buzzing with news. Death in Iraq. Black sites. Anthrax. Wiretapping. Backpacks zipped, jackets lost and found. "Where's your homework?" The congested kitchen throbbed with activity. "Put your shoes on." Yellow cake uranium. I made sandwiches and folded napkins for packed lunches. Suicide bombers. "No, there's no time to use the computer, Charlie. It's time for school." I kissed my children and wife goodbye before they rushed out the door, all three of them, click-click-click. And then it was just the two of us again, this puppy and me.

Tex watched me scoop hard brown pellets of food into his bowl. Bending to his will, I served him as if he were my master, but he did not appear grateful for this service. He regarded my compliance as his birthright.

For the first time in my life I questioned the practice of electing a pet dog. The whole system seemed flawed to me. You might as well invite a highway drifter into your home and handcuff yourself to him for eight years. You feed him a gross ton of food, which he summarily craps out on your floor or on your lawn. You always have to clean up after him. The quiet neighbors complain about his barking. More often than not he doesn't even come when you call him. I could go on, but I think the case has been made.

At ten o'clock that morning, Tex sauntered through the living room without a care in the world. Now, I want it noted for the permanent record that I'm no expert on canine genitalia, but I believe that anyone, including innocent children and the elderly, would have shared my shock at the sight of the private parts swinging between his stumpy legs. Had Tex been sired by a caribou? I was tempted to put a pair of Bermuda shorts on him just so that I could finish my Cheerios in peace.

Our neighbors grew to hate him. Every time I released him to the outdoors he immediately shat on their lawns, bit off the heads of their flowers, and made so much noise that they threat-ened to call the police. "He's your dog," they said.

"No, he's not," I said. "He just showed up on our door-step."

I had once enjoyed a sterling reputation on our cul-de-sac. I was widely considered one of the most enthusiastic members of our Neighborhood Watch committee. I was known for my smile, the booming hello I offered everyone, my willingness to pitch in on community initiatives. Those days were forgotten. The people who used to pat Willy's head and rub his belly while Willy rolled in the grass with his legs in the air were now form-ing coalitions against my family, against me.

I missed another day of work. I called Manny and explained that we had a new puppy in the house. I was involved in a domestic dilemma, I said, and would need to take a few more days off. "You're just digging yourself deeper and deeper," he said, and handed the phone to Wren, a part-time employee with no previous references and shaky intrapersonal skills.

In a moment of weakness, I told Wren about Tex. Amaz-ingly, Wren's voice became bright and lively. She said that she understood completely. She was a cat owner, a cat caregiver, and things could get hairy. Sometimes ignoring domesticated animals was the best policy, Wren advised.

If simply ignoring Tex proved ineffective, Wren suggested a ten-minute Time Out in the locked bathroom. "See if that doesn't change his tune," she said with a laugh.

I never knew Wren had such strong, interesting ideas on this topic. At her desk, she wore elbow-length satin gloves from the Goodwill. Her hair changed colors almost every week. She wore torn fishnets and platform boots. A kitten-on-a-rope poster hung in her cubicle—"Hang in there," it said—but Wren had redacted "in there" with a black sharpie. Once, I watched her chop all the hair off the rubber troll on her pencil and put the shimmering purple strands in the suggestion box. She winked at me and said, "I hope they consider it." I laughed like a broken bell; I both did and did not understand what she meant. Her laugh sounded like an ambulance siren. Earlier in the week I'd noticed her inner thigh tattoo of the Virgin Mary. I stared at it for too long.

Wren continued to advise me. We had never talked much before, and it excited me to hear her voice in my ear. She said if her last suggestion didn't prove to be an effective anger-management technique and Tex continued to act out, then I should consider a strategic food withdrawal followed by sleep deprivation. "Keep all the lights on in his room and play glam rock at full blast," she said. "We're talking Winger, Bon Jovi, Poison. He'll know who's boss then." She gave me her cell number and told me to text any new developments.

I thanked her for her input, but I did not lock up Tex or deny him the comforts of food and sleep. That wasn't my style. I believed in reaching accord through means of diplomacy, compromise, and empathy.

The conflict only intensified. Tex mangled my favorite pair of running shoes. He chewed up a half dozen paperbacks in my bookcase and reduced my favorite bathrobe to soggy shreds of plaid flannel. At night I couldn't sleep or get comfortable in bed. Mary Ellen couldn't stand my fidgeting and sighing. She asked me to please take my pillow to the couch downstairs.

"But I want to sleep with you," I told her.

"Just for tonight," she said and handed me my pillow. "I need a little space."

Tex was tickled by this turn of events. He peeked out from the comfort of his bedroom and stared at me, a big stupid grin on his face. It was impossible to deny his popularity. Nothing short of a scandal would have diminished his luster. But he was too careful, too folksy about his mishaps, too cute to fail.

Exiled on the couch, unable to sleep, I plotted a coup. I didn't need anybody's help, I decided. There would be no paper trail. No more calls to Wren. I could handle this one myself.

In the living room, Tex and I stared at each other like gunslingers in a Western.

"I see what you're doing." I propped myself on one elbow. "You hope to bring ruin upon this family, but you won't get away with it. You may have fooled my wife and kids, but I know you're a fake, and public opinion is turning. Our neighbors are on to you. You're not nearly as clever as you think. The mask will soon crack."

Tex didn't reply. He looked at me without pity or remorse. Then he returned to his room and nudged the door shut with his snout.

Early the following morning I awakened from a dead sleep and knew what to do. The plan had come to me in a dream.

Before my family stirred, I shredded a dishtowel, overturned a lamp, and perforated a student paper of Mary Ellen's with my own slobbery teeth marks. I scattered the pages about. Then I bit a doggie biscuit in half, leaving one piece on the floor by the couch and swallowing the other half, thereby destroying the evidence. I ground one of Charlie's favorite video games under my boot heel, destroying it completely. I ripped the blonde hair out of Alice's favorite doll and flung the synthetic strands on the carpet.

Finally, in a stroke of genius, I wrote a quick note on a pink Post-It. "Went out for delicious donuts for the family I love. Back in 20 mins. Love, Daddy."

Was that enough? I worried that it was not enough. So I urinated on my wife's cardigan sweater, the one she wore around the house a few times a week. I'd given it to her three years earlier and was surprised and pleased by how much she adored it. I was saddened to see it defaced by Tex.

Still, I wasn't sure they would see it my way, so I made the executive decision to defecate on our couch.

I'll confess to a moment of uncertainty. Should I have taken a different approach to incentivize my team? We all had a lot on our plates that quarter. Mary Ellen was so deep in the weeds with those student papers you couldn't see her face anymore. The kids were giving as good as they got. Somebody needed to push the envelope. We couldn't let the grass grow on this one. In a family such as ours, the team leader had to do some heavy lifting to stay one step ahead of the paradigm shifts. I completed my davenport project in record time, hurried to the bathroom and performed the necessary ablutions.

A minute later, I banged on the puppy's bedroom door. "Wake up. Wake up, you adorable little sleepyhead." Tex tore out of his room barking like a maniac. He dove for my ankles, snapping with his sharp teeth, but I danced out of the way. "Ha, ha, ha." Taunting him with my laughter, I ran circles around the soiled couch. Tex leaped onto the cushions. His right front paw landed squarely in my feces. He jumped back down and ran around the room, smearing it all over the carpet.

Game, set, match: Daddy.

"Bye, bye," I said and hurried out the door.

I rang the front doorbell to wake up the family, pulled out of the attached garage, and drove away laughing.

When Mary Ellen saw that disgusting mess, she would be outraged, horrified. She'd finally realize what a terrible mistake she'd made. Even the kids would be revolted. They'd cover their mouths and run around in circles, going, "Ewww! Tex made weewee on Mommy's sweater and doodoo on the couch." And twenty minutes later, Daddy would reappear, all smiles and innocence, the returning hero, carrying a bright pink and orange box filled with fresh delicious donuts. Greeted by pandemonium, Daddy would march in and restore order.

I would prevent Mary Ellen from cleaning it up herself. "Let me do it," I'd volunteer, a no-brainer considering the origin of the mess. "You shouldn't have to put up with this." Donning yellow dishwashing gloves with surgeon-like confidence, I would both instigate the cleanup efforts and delegate responsibilities. "Kids, go in the kitchen and have some donuts. I bought all your favorites." And to Mary Ellen: "Make no mistake. After I clean up here, we'll go out and buy a new couch. Any style you want. Your choice."

Later that afternoon Tex would be tried and convicted as a war criminal. Soon he would be out of our lives forever.

First, though, we'd sit down as a loving family and enjoy the donuts that wonderful Daddy had brought home. We would laugh and celebrate. Then we'd have our last family meeting. There would be some new business to discuss. I expected the vote to be unanimous. That puppy wouldn't know what hit him, and peace would be restored at last.

For the first time in my life, I drove the long way to the shopping plaza, leaving behind all the cottage houses with their narrow lawns and short driveways. I hit all the red lights but couldn't stop smiling. Confident that I'd taken care of everything at home, I turned up the radio as loud as it would go. Hard rock blared from the speakers. I lowered the driver's side window and pounded my palms on the steering wheel. I shouted at a jaywalker: "Let's keep it moving!"

Carried away by all the excitement, I gripped the wheel in one hand and called my coworker, Wren, on her cell phone. "You'll never guess what I just did."

Wren asked me if I wanted to come over to her apartment. She said she was frying eggs and drinking vodka.

That sounded like a dangerous and inadvisable situation.

"See you soon," I said.

HALLIE BANG

That summer I had been reading *Steppenwolf,* and at night I walked around town in cutoffs and a Hawaiian shirt, thinking about despair, not sure if I was actually in it myself, and one Friday night, on a whim, I ended up at J.P. Bullfeathers on Elmwood Avenue, where I drank draft beer at the bar and watched a dull boxing match on the muted TV above the cash register. Waitresses hurried by with steak tacos and chicken wings for the bikers on the front patio. Around 11:30, just as I was leaving, my old friends Cheryl and Carlos rolled in, drunk and laughing, with funny stories to tell. So I hung out with them, chain-drinking beers and throwing plastic darts. Around midnight a troupe of modern dancers flapped into the bar like tropical birds that had migrated to the rust belt by mistake. They were still in their stage costumes—flowing dresses and head wraps—and I recognized a guy I knew, John Cogan, grinning in the midst of them. The women disappeared into the back room of the bar where there were tables, and John and I shook hands, stood by the front windows and talked shit about *The Cracked Bowl,* a tiny local journal we both had poems published in, and after a while one of the dancers came up to him and said, "John, we're all waiting for you in the back, we're gonna order food soon," and he said OK, then he introduced us. Buffalo is not a big city and I had seen her around on Elmwood Avenue—long straight copper hair and a pale lovely face and a nose ring and skinny arms and legs and a walk that at times seemed more like hopping—and I had read a poem of hers in *The Cracked Bowl*, back when I used to study each issue in secret devotion, hoping that someday a poem of mine would appear in it. So when John said, "Do you know Hallie Bang? She had a poem in the *Bowl* a while ago," I said, "Yes, I know," and recited a few lines for her on the spot. I had remembered it, I don't know why. She stared at me, frowned, and said nothing, then returned to her friends. An hour later I was pounding tequila shots with Cheryl and Carlos and Hallie came out of the back room, plopped down on a stool near me, and ordered a beer. We started shouting at each other over the music. Hallie flailed her hands and laughed as she talked, gray-green eyes, nose ring glinting, and I wanted her phone number, but she took off while I was in the men's room. That week there was a reading for the latest *Cracked Bowl* and I was scooping some fruit chunks onto my paper plate—pineapples, melons—and John Cogan said, "You're popular all of a sudden. Two women have been asking about you," and I said, "Is one of them Hallie Bang?" and he said, "Yeah," and I said, "Well then I don't care who the other one is." I read my crappy poem that night, one that took me two years to write, and then John, Hallie Bang, her roommate Annie and I went to the Old Pink to get drunk. We shot a few games of pool, and I told a story that made Hallie spit her vodka tonic onto Annie, laughing, but when John offered me a ride home, I declined. They all piled into his Monte Carlo and I started heading back to my apartment on Lafayette and Grant, a half hour walk. John slowed his rumbling Chevy beside me. "You don't want a ride, man? Hop in." Hallie and Annie looked out at me from the passenger side windows. I shook my head. "Thanks, anyway!" Now I understand that I had painted a confusing picture of myself in Hallie's eyes—a man walking home alone with a depressing novel hidden in the baggy pocket of his bermudas—but the truth is I was insecure and could conceal my awkwardness for only a few hours at a time. I had to get away from them, I thought, before I blew it and turned into a monster of unease. I went home that night and talked about this odd, brilliant, beautiful Hallie Bang to my roommate. There wasn't much to say—I didn't know her—but I managed to talk a lot. He yawned and wondered why the hell I didn't get her phone number. I was twenty years old and still couldn't recognize when a woman was attracted to me. Any signs of encouragement were imaginary, I believed, wishful thinking on my part and not to be acted upon. About a week later, I think, Hallie called me up and asked me out for coffee. That night I had plans with Jodi, the stoner who lived on the first floor of my building, but I said yes to Hallie anyway—hence our future joke that we both dumped our Jodis for each other. Her Jodi was actually named Steve. We agreed to meet at Pano's, a Greek diner on Elmwood: four greasy booths and a cracked counter with maybe nine squeaky stools. Intimate, grubby, perfect. I arrived first and tried to read my book, but I was too keyed-up to concentrate. Then Hallie meandered in, twenty minutes late, glowing in bright colors—orange and green and purple. Her clothes looked like they'd been knitted by a blind person. She wasn't a jeans and T-shirt type of woman. She wore a scarf on her head and yellow combat boots, and I would give anything to experience that same fear and elation again, the feeling that we were starting something new together. Hallie drank her coffee black, one sugar, but she peeled back the lids of two half-and-half containers and tossed them down her throat as if they were shots of whiskey and she were a sailor on shore leave. I laughed. "What?" she said. "You've never done this before? It tastes like melted vanilla ice cream." She made me take a shot and watched my reaction. "Like melted vanilla ice cream," I said. "Right!" she said. "That's what I think, too." I ordered a chicken souvlaki and Hallie got a buttered pita bulging with scrambled eggs and feta cheese. Halfway through the meal I ran out to buy a bottle of red wine at the liquor store down the street. Throughout our meal, people kept coming up to the table and talking to Hallie. Every time it happened I had a mouth full of souvlaki. She introduced me to Yousouff, Suki, Elise, Dagoberto, Amy. I couldn't keep the names straight. Even the short order cook acknowledged her with a nod and sent over a flaky brick of baklava. "Where do you know all these people from?" I asked her. Not one person had come up to the table to talk to me. Hallie shrugged and said she hadn't thought about it before. She lived in a small world full of people who loved her, people who made squealing noises when they saw her. Nobody received more hugs in a day than Hallie Bang. Our waitress, who also knew Hallie from somewhere, gave us empty coffee mugs for our wine, and she didn't seem to care that we sat there for two hours drinking. So we brought in a second bottle of wine and poured a third mug for our waitress, who stored hers under the counter. When I paid for our meals I left a hundred percent tip, pretending money wasn't an issue. Money was definitely an issue for me. Outside Pano's a palm reader sat behind a card table, and I paid for two readings. I can't remember a single thing the fortuneteller said, though I do remember tipping her five extra bucks, and Hallie and I wandered in the general direction of her apartment. Whether the creases in our palms predicted our futures or marked the history of everything we'd held and let go, I couldn't imagine a better purpose for my right paw, and its elaborate framework of little bones, muscles and nerves, than when it closed the space between us and grasped Hallie's small hand, linking us for four blocks while we practically skipped down the sidewalk. Outside her apartment I said good night and offered her a handshake. "Really?" Hallie said. "That's what we're doing? Try again." So I pressed her up against the wall and kissed her. When our tongues met, her hands rummaged beneath my shirt, her hot fingers on my lower back. I kissed her neck just under her ear, both of my hands in her hair, and then I followed her up the rotting wooden stairs to her third-floor apartment. Her mattress was under a dormer window in the living room. Her roommate Annie slept in the apartment's one bedroom, which you had to pass through to use the slant-ceilinged bathroom, and everywhere on the hardwood floor and on cluttered counters were the props of their interesting lives—paintings on canvas and wood, stretcher bars and sketches, tackle boxes filled with charcoals and pencils and books everywhere, a cheap acoustic guitar missing its bottom E string, and broken pottery and dirty plates. "Who plays guitar?" I asked. Hallie grabbed the back of my head and kissed me. She sucked on my lower lip and pushed me back against the couch and straddled my hips. I had only been with one girl before, my high school girlfriend, but this felt different to me. I scooped Hallie up—her body vined around mine, her arms around my neck, her ankles crossed behind my thighs—and I carried her across the room and flung her down on the lumpy mattress. We undressed each other. She bit my shoulder, hard. When I kissed her belly and continued to descend, she took hold of my head and almost tore off my ears, bucked her hips hard into my face, and I thought, Tear them off. I don't need ears, don't need eyes, and you can break my nose because I want to feel it all, and I'm staying right here until you push me away, until you've had enough. Her breathing turned crazy. Finally she rolled away from me, twitching, before turning back again. She climbed on top of me and guided me into her. Then she jabbed the heels of her hands so hard into my shoulders, and she rocked, her eyes closed, thinking whatever. I held on to her. Eventually, her eyes popped open, and she looked down, as if she was surprised to see me there. When she lowered her face to mine, I thought she might ask me who I was. Instead, she kissed my cheek, my neck, where I felt her breath, her tongue and lips, and for the first time I trusted that there might be something real between us, but I couldn't quite say yet what it was. Afterward, I wound a strand of copper hair around my wrist while she talked about her half-sister, and I could hear the way she felt about the people she loved. The only downside to any of this was her jealous cat, General Sow. He patrolled the perimeter of the apartment like a sadistic prison guard hoping that one of his inmates would step out of line. More than once I turned to find this fat cat stalking me, creeping up on me to slash my balls with his dagger claws while I lay naked in bed. But I made it through the night without injury and the following morning Hallie and Annie sang and played guitar, and I knew then that they could cut an album if they'd only write more songs, but they had five songs, that was it, and they were beautiful, and we spent another day in bed while Annie worked her shift at the co-op, and that evening when Hallie made dinner she asked me to help and I didn't know what to do with an eggplant, but I faked it and maybe it was endearing, who knows, and we started spending whole days together, loitering on Allen Street or in the park, and when it got too hot outdoors we crashed at her place, listening to her Phoebe Snow and Roberta Flack albums, and napping in that bed under the whooshing trees, and the road crew outside her apartment showed up every morning at 8:00 a.m., causing Hallie to whisper in my ear, "Oh, the chirping of the jackhammers fills my heart with joy." Sometimes Hallie knew what I was thinking before I did, recognized when I was wandering off into the wildwood of my mind, second-guessing myself—"turning into a pretzel," she called it, and she poked her finger into my forehead and said, "*Dzzzzt*," as if to change the frequency of my brain waves, a perfect shorthand gesture that never failed to bring me back to the present. "My parents were lunatics, Hallie. Totally incompetent. Why did they even have kids?" "*Dzzzzt*." Finger to the forehead. "Look at this, babe. I'm definitely going bald." "*Dzzzzt*." Right between the eyes. It's no small thing to say why you love someone. I have always thought it a worthy goal, however impossible. Sometimes Hallie counted my ribs—one, two, three—or she compared the circumferences of our thighs with her cupped hands. Constant physical contact, breath-sniffing closeness, seemed crucial to her. Four days a week I rode my bike to work thinking of Hallie Bang and the things she said, and I couldn't wait to get back to her apartment, where there was no TV so we played Hallie-invented games like "Wear It!" which meant you had to heap as many items on your body as you could, including T-shirts, sweaters, winter coats, scarves, clip-on key chains, clothes hangers, and whatever else was within reach. I won this game of hers only once, when I picked up the shocked General Sow and wore him like a stole. Other nights we sat cross-legged on her bed in our underwear and played cards, Crazy Eights, or I read my favorite authors to her, and then we looked at her weird penis sculpture for a while, an activity always followed by intense, ardent sex—sweat shining on sunburned skin, her sheets a twisted braid on the floor—and Hallie knocked on Annie's door once, saying, "We're going for a walk now," and Annie joked back, "*Can* you guys walk after that?" and we headed toward Delaware Park and got stuck in the rain and it didn't matter and the smell of grass is in my mind now and I'm sniffing the air because I smell that summer and I have never wanted anyone to like me more than I wanted her to. In July, she went to North Carolina to dance at the American Dance Festival but we talked on the phone almost every day, and one weekend I flew into Raleigh-Durham Airport as a surprise, riding around Duke University campus in a green-and-white cab for thirty minutes until I found the address she had given me, and I hurled peppermints at the window of the white brick building she inhabited with five other dancers, and for two nights we shared a mummy bag on the cement floor, until I was politely told to leave by a stern, gray-haired woman named Mrs. Turco. That August Hallie's roommate Annie went to Chicago for graduate school, so Hallie moved into my apartment and we cooked meals together and drank coffee at midnight and walked around town, and she sniffed and tasted and touched everything she could get her hands on and pointed at things and made up stories about them, and once when I came home from work on my bike she had choreographed the neighborhood kids to ambush me with water pistols and they piled out of bushes and nearby garages drenching me to the skin while Hallie sat watching from our porch and laughed, and I began to think about marriage and children of our own, thoughts that didn't scare me at all, and I gave her two drawers in my dresser and half my closet, and we had sex everywhere in that apartment—on the floor, in the shower, in my bed, on my roommate's bed—and we lived in three more places together, two in Brooklyn and a hovel in Paris, where she had a difficult abortion, not wanting to jeopardize her dancing career, a decision I supported, and I started bartending at La Violon Dingue, where I drank for free every night and got paid under the table, and she met a new bunch of friends who loved her, a troupe of Czech dancers who performed on the streets of Pigalle and passed the hat to tourists, the two of us staying out nights, lying to each other, bored with each other, fighting about nothing, until one morning we passed in the kitchen like any two strangers on Elmwood Avenue might, and that was that.

IS THE VAGINA NECESSARY?

My work on the vagina is well known, both nationally and internationally. I have been an expert in this field for over seventeen years. At a recent academic conference in Houston, I presented my peer-reviewed article, "Vaginas After Adorno: The Legacy of Pseudo Individualism in a Gendered World." Then I fielded some fascinating questions from the audience. "How does the vagina affect industry in a post-industrial age?" one curious man wanted to know. "What were the newest innovations, if any, in the vagina field?" asked another man. And most importantly: "Is the vagina really necessary, after all?" I enjoyed being in the presence of these scholars, my peers. They were polite, erudite, elderly, drunk.

My morning panel started out strong. The first two presenters were enthusiastic and delivered their papers with commendable vigor. After thirty minutes, though, I sensed a slight deflation of energy in the room. Their exuberance soon petered out. How much could you really say about this subject? Yes, you could dress it up this way and that, perhaps let Marx and Freud and Foucault take a few whacks at the vagina, which could land you in sticky territory these days, but at the end of the day we were all just regurgitating the same old facts. Many of my colleagues seemed eager to move on to the buffet luncheon and put the whole question behind us.

Before I began reading my paper, I looked out at the audience. A few of the older scholars nodded off in the front row. They slumped in their seats and snored like infants. Their gray stubbly chins bounced gently on their chests. I raised my voice to combat the hum, but a new commotion kicked up. Somebody had turned on a portable TV in the back of the room. Heads turned in that direction. Chairs scraped on the floor. The vagina, I'm afraid, was already forgotten.

Hell, I knew it was a dry topic, but as the morning's keynote speaker, I had an obligation to arouse and titillate my audience. I spoke in a folksy tone of voice without the aid of notes or a PowerPoint presentation. I opened with a few ribald jokes to help loosen things up. Somebody lowered the volume on the TV. I held everybody's interest when I talked about the inherently faulty structure of the vagina, how it contained numerous design flaws and could be easily fortified and weatherproofed. This concept intrigued my colleagues.

"Girders?" a man suggested from the back of the room. He held the TV's remote control in his hand. "What if we added girders?"

My first thought was no. Girders were not the answer. That type of sweeping change would require, at the very least, permits, and most likely congressional hearings, and perhaps even an amendment to the Constitution. But I didn't want him to hit the volume again, so I pretended to take his suggestion under advisement. And as the morning wore on I sat with it, played with it. Nobody had spoken up against him or proposed an alternative. In time his suggestion seemed unassailable to us. By 11:35 a.m. we all agreed that girders could and should be implemented in the vagina. There would be dangers, but we were not concerned about that. One couldn't make an omelet without cracking a few—

But then a young surgeon from Tulsa stood up and explained the physiological difficulties. He seemed to know what he was talking about. It demoralized us. We were back at square one with the old-model vagina, the same one women have been lugging around since time immemorial. We were, after all, trying to help them, women, and girls, too. We worked hard at this annual conference to improve their lives, so even though we'd hit a temporary snag, we weren't prepared to admit defeat.

"I say we install cameras," a man from Denver suggested during the spirited Q & A session that followed my talk, "so we can always know what's all up in there. Especially when we're not around to monitor them ourselves."

We chuckled. This gentleman sounded a bit radical for my taste, but he had a point. Our actual face-to-face interaction with the vagina, compared with the inordinate amount of time we spent in our cars or at the gym, was minimal, bordering on nonexistent. Women could have been doing all kinds of funky things with those vaginas when we weren't looking. Nevertheless, we understood and fully respected that some folks became nervous about surveillance and nobody, I mean nobody, cared more about civil liberties than scholars like myself, a full professor for over two decades with numerous teaching awards under my belt. Another participant talked about recent innovations in chastity belts, a medieval apparatus now gaining popularity in the BDSM community, but I found the topic distasteful and silenced his voice using the power of my microphone, my amplified voice, and my credentials. Nobody questioned my credentials. The man withdrew into himself, and rightly so. We decided to break for lunch.

On a personal note, this vagina conference is always a thrill for me. It's my favorite week of the year. Frankly, it's invigorating to get out of the classroom and into the real world of a convention center. The vagina conference allows me to catch up with my peers, to familiarize myself with cutting-edge research, and to experience life as it's really lived off the college campus.

So we broke for lunch in high spirits, feeling productive, but the smoked brisket, unfortunately, was chewy and bland, and the potatoes were cold. I didn't want to be branded a malcontent and miss out on next year's conference in Maui, so I said nothing about the provender, but the man seated next to me angrily filled out a complaint card. When I saw that he intended to sign his own name, I reminded him that the waitstaff took their sweet time refilling our coffee cups. He thanked me and added that condemnation as a footnote.

Well, now, okay, I suppose I've danced around "the incident" long enough. I have to admit I'm trying to put a positive spin on the conference, in case any of my colleagues read this think piece, but a strange thing happened at this year's conference in Houston, and I'd be remiss if I didn't touch on it.

In the Men's room, just after the subpar brisket lunch and minutes before I returned to kick off the second half of the day's program, I had a brief but shocking crisis of conscience at the urinal. I questioned my own authority. When all was said and done, what did I really know about the vagina? Although I was a confirmed expert in my field (my numerous publications attest to this, not to mention my Gender Studies degree from Duke), wasn't it true that I had never known what it was like to *own* a vagina—that is to say, to tune-up and maintain a vagina on an hour-to-hour basis? I had not grown up with one, had not nurtured it through multiple disappointments, had not celebrated its numerous triumphs. I had never once applied a soothing balm, nor had I sung to my vagina a German lullaby such as *"Der Hahn is tot"* or *"Fingerspiel von der Familie,"* as I imagined most women did at night when their vaginas were distressed by the day's events.

I frowned at my face in that Men's room mirror, fearing that I was an impostor and had no right to speak as a vagina specialist at the Houston Sheraton. As I washed my hands, I lost confidence in the second paper I'd soon be sharing with my colleagues, "The Dialectics of Vaginal Hegemony: A Cultural Praxis." My opinions on women's issues seemed—for that one painful moment at the mirror—flimsy, inconsequential, and unethical.

For more than a minute I considered the radical act of not delivering my paper at all, not speaking on the topic at hand, but rather asking questions instead, placing myself in the subservient role of the student and becoming "teachable." Then I washed my hands. The life of the academic, as we all know, is fraught with such moments of doubt. Practically every evening we have to push through our suspicions of fraudulence, usually with the aid of alcoholic lubricants.

Minutes later, I strode into the conference room with my shoulders back, my pocket square sharp as a knife. I hit the stage running. "Let's get it started," I called out, rotating my fist above my head. "Woot, woot, woot."

The older gentlemen, it should be noted, were counting on me for energy. In their eyes, I was a spry fifty-nine-year-old progressive who brought a spark of defiance to my field. In fact, they still called me The Kid, a handle that tickled me. Here I'd been flown into Houston (at no small expense to the university where I hold an endowed chair) to discuss the contemporary American vagina primarily, to shed light on this murky and controversial subject, while touching briefly on the Global Vagina and the Vagina of Emerging Nations (you really can't get around it these days, but you have to wear kid gloves), and that's exactly what I intended to do. This conference provided us all with the consistency we appreciated: a few laughs, a few questions, maybe a tepid argument resolved with a handshake or even a fist bump. Afterward, we'd grab a nice dinner at the hotel and maybe catch part of the jazz show in the hotel bar, where the drinks flowed well past 11:00 p.m.

As I said, I brought top-notch enthusiasm to the stage that afternoon, but almost as soon as I entered the conference room, I noticed a disturbing trend. The men in the room were less receptive to the topic after lunch. It seemed like they didn't want to think about the historical vagina at all. They yawned rudely without covering their mouths, and completely ignored my PowerPoint presentation.

That might have been the low point of the conference for me had there not been an unexpected disruption. A new attendee, a first-timer named "Hal," stood up during my précis on the antebellum vagina, tore the salt-and-pepper wig off his head, stripped off his handsome blazer, and revealed himself to be an impostor. We were shocked and appalled by the protrusions stretching out his shirtfront.

"Give me that microphone," Hal said in a shockingly high-pitched voice. It was then that I realized that Hal was not a man after all. He, I mean, *she* was on the stage before I could react and snatched the microphone out of my hand. "You all value abstract terminology higher than common sense."

All the other men at Hal's table stood up and disrobed. I determined, after a moment of peering over my bifocals, that these six were not gentlemen either. There were now seven women in the room. A note on our conference: we had never once excluded women. They were welcome to submit papers, and many of them did. It was simply a statistical anomaly that none of them had been invited to present their work before us.

The intruder motioned to her crotch with the microphone. "The 'historical vagina,' as you call it, is with us here today. The entire history of the vagina is right here, boys. Look no further."

"Fascinating theory," I said, leaning over and speaking into her microphone, my microphone, knowing that the men were counting on me to remain unruffled, "but let's leave your little vagina out of this and move on to—"

"Careful, pal," she said, aiming the cocked gun of her finger at me. "My vagina never did anything wrong to you." She glared at me. Then she paused and took a breath. "My vagina and I have been through quite a bit together," she said, her voice amplified in all four corners of the room. "We have traveled the world together. Paris, Detroit, Anchorage, Hanoi, so many memories." She laughed quietly to herself. The other women grinned, perhaps recalling their own high points with their vaginas.

I felt out of my depths for a moment. My scholarly work had been anthologized and widely admired, true, and several awards for pedagogical expertise had confirmed what I had always thought about myself, but I'd never seen anything like this before, and I didn't appreciate how this dislocation made me feel.

In an attempt to restore order, I continued addressing my audience. "Let's shift our focus, gentlemen, to the twentieth century—"

"Enough!" said the woman with the microphone. "You know, I had hoped it wouldn't come to this. But you forced my hand, sir. You don't know the first thing about the vagina."

With malice aforethought, these seven trespassers began to unbuckle their belts, to unzip their slacks, to hike up their skirts and dresses. We were frightened by the threat of what we might witness under the fluorescent lights. We blushed and turned our heads. A pale septuagenarian in the front row clutched his chest. It had been over twenty years since he'd seen one outside the pages of a book. His neighbor, a heavyset scholar in his mid-fifties, waved a handkerchief over the old man's face and said, "Ma'am, you're killing the chair of my department."

None of us was prepared for something like this. The intrusion was shocking. We would have liked advanced warning—a "trigger warning" as the kids call it nowadays—and perhaps the option to down a few cocktails first. We would have appreciated the option to say no or yes. This was a lurid and inappropriate display, a spectacle to be countenanced only behind closed doors, under the covers of a marital bed or a hotel room, in the secret dark, not during an academic conference in the broad daylight of Houston, Texas, the taste of barbecued brisket still in our mouths. We couldn't turn the page, nor could we hit a button on the keyboard. This was real, this was shocking, this was sudden, this was illegal.

"We are not here to see *that*," I complained, unable to conceal the childlike whine in my voice. I spoke through tightly clenched lips. "We are here to talk about the conceptual nature of the vagina. That is all."

"This is it," she said, pointing to her still-clothed crotch. "What more do you need to know?"

"This has gone too far," I said. "Have you no shame, madam? We are not here to indulge in pornography."

I motioned to the security guards. Two bulky male students—scholarship boys who were fulfilling their work-study obligations—began inching toward the interlopers but kept a respectful distance. Dressed in matching red golf shirts and black slacks, the word SECURITY embossed on their backs, the boys approached with darting eyes, hands open at their sides, clearly unprepared for this incursion. None of us knew what to do next.

The woman with the microphone said, "But why does this vagina scare you? Why do you feel the need to govern *this*?"

I checked my notes. I flipped through the pages hoping to land on a rebuttal.

"Gender is a social construct," she said to me. "That's all. Dude, stop looking at your notes and listen to me for one second."

Grudgingly, I gave her my attention.

"You've been conditioned by a system that imprisons your thoughts and actions," she said. "You've been commodified. Break free, man. Break *out*."

I flipped through all nineteen pages of my paper, looking for a relevant quote with which to rebut her hysterical arguments. Marx, I thought, would help me. Surely Karl Marx could carry me through this predicament. Hadn't we all found clever ways to ignore his secret sexual liaison with his own housekeeper, the laborer he employed, in order to admire his groundbreaking ideas about the working class? Or Freud, I thought. Save me, Uncle Siggie. Okay, yes, he'd made a few mistakes with Dora and also believed the vagina to be a tomb that symbolically represented the absence of a penis, but I was certain he'd written sensibly, rationally, coldly, about this very topic. The only way to combat this woman's outsized emotions was to perform an object lesson in stone-cold logic. My notes appeared to me as if they'd been written in a foreign language. The words literally blurred before my eyes and became unreadable. Sweat broke out on my high forehead. I had almost conceded defeat. But, but, but, in the end, I knew, this was a job for Michel Foucault, bald, beautiful, masculine, academic as hell, a thinker who focused on the relationship between power and the body. Her microphone-seizing gambit was a power play, pure and simple, and only Foucault could save us from it.

"There is no power relation without the correlative constitution of a field of knowledge," I shrieked, quoting *Discipline and Punish*, "nor any knowledge that does not presuppose and constitute at the same time power relations."

My colleagues breathed a collective sigh of relief. Here was the soothing balm of academic jargon, sweet jargon, here was the brain asserting dominance over the body, the intellect governing feeling. We were out of the bordello and back in the classroom, where all the unpredictable heat and spontaneity of the body was safely quarantined, hidden, repressed, contextualized.

I had found my voice. My back straightened and my legs felt steady beneath me. "Resistances do not derive from a few heterogeneous principles," I said, now quoting from Foucault's *History of Sexuality*, flexing my fifty-nine-year-old muscles a bit, I admit, "but neither are they a lure or a promise that is of necessity betrayed. They are the odd term in relations of power; they are inscribed in the latter as an irreducible opposite."

The woman with the microphone laughed. That's all. She just laughed, an act of brutality. She registered the sweat on my glazed forehead, the terror in my eyes of being exposed as a fraud, the quaver in my whiskey-textured baritone voice, the liver spots on my hands, my pot belly barely concealed by dress shirt and tie, my penis defenseless as a mushroom cap in a bog of moss, and she simply, carelessly, cruelly laughed at me, as though I were nothing more than a turbulent child.

"Are you laughing at me?" I asked.

She smiled. That smile shattered me. She knew it right then and there, knew exactly what she had accomplished, and didn't have to say another word. Her pitying smile pierced me more deeply than any steel or lead weapon ever could. Her presence alone had altered the conference forever. I felt as though she were looking at an old oil painting on the wall of an empty museum, a quaint but meaningless artifact. She handed me the microphone and turned back to her collaborators.

They returned to their table, no longer in disguise, and waited for me to deliver my presentation. The words caught in my throat. I couldn't understand a single word of what I had written. I looked out at the audience, unable to ignore the presence in the front row. My throat was a desert, my brain a broken toy.

My inquisitor took pity on me. "We don't intend to cause any more trouble here today," she called out. "Let's go, gals. We'll be at the bar if you need us or want to continue this discussion in a civil manner."

I watched them leave, filing out of the room with dignity and grace. The old men in the audience looked to me with drowning eyes. They hoped I could put the experience into context. As a representative of the next generation, I owed it to them to carry our cherished ideals into the future. A good leader would have synthesized the relevant materials and situated them historically. He would have soldiered ahead without even acknowledging the disturbance or he would have stitched the crisis into the fabric of his own argument.

But I was not up to the task. Instead I watched the impostors depart through the back door. They were still smiling, laughing, unburdened.

I abandoned my notes on the lectern. I removed my nametag, dismounted from the stage, and hustled through the conference room with my eyes lowered, skirting between the tables and chairs, straining to overhear their conversation as they filed out the back door. Men reached out to pat me on the back, trying to console me, but I shook them off. These women had answers to questions I'd never asked. I longed to join them at the bar to listen, to hear what they had to say. Nothing in my life seemed more important. The world was changing. Only a fool would have ignored it. What a great resource women could be for my next book! I could probe them for specifics and pass their insights off as my own.

Just before I exited, though, a man cried out, "Joists! We haven't mentioned joists. That might solve our structural problem."

I confess I was intrigued. So I hung around a little longer, eager to hear what the other scholars, my peers, would say in response.

BENEFACTOR

The man who teaches me to see with new eyes what I see
everyday—that man is my benefactor.

—Paul Valéry

This is how Parker broke into the art world. He was on his couch, eating a salami sandwich, when a captivating woman appeared on his TV screen. "For only nineteen ninety-nine a month," she said, "you too can adopt an impoverished artist. Help keep some struggling painter or sculptor alive in this economic downturn. These artists truly need your help, friends. Just look at this poor fellow."

A man in a Slayer T-shirt and denim shorts limped into the frame. His pitted, unshaved face was etched with years of suffering. Scraggly hair, sad tattoos. The woman, an actor in her late twenties, held her ground with admirable dignity, ignoring what must have been a heady stench. Her clean auburn hair was pinned up on her head, as if she had a dinner party to attend after taping this promo. Parker sat forward on his couch, transfixed.

"Help end the suffering, friends," she said. "This artist needs a sponsor like you." Still smiling, she turned and placed her regal white hand on the man's shoulder.

"Careful," Parker said to her, now sitting on the edge of the couch, hammered after another night of solitary drinking.

"Can you find it in your heart to change this man's luck?" she said, looking directly into the camera. "Please give now. Operators are standing by."

Before he knew it, Parker had his phone in one hand and his credit card in the other. He laid his half eaten sandwich on the arm of the couch. "I want an artist," he said to the toll-free operator. "That's what I need. Definitely."

The operator wasted no time in gathering the necessary data. "Congratulations, sir. You've made the right decision. May I have your name, please, and your credit card information?"

Two weeks later, the first of several information packets appeared in his mailbox. Parker learned that Gerry "The Balls" Husk, his adopted artist, was a forty-seven-year-old "up and comer" who was currently crashing on a buddy's futon in Red Hook. Because he couldn't afford to buy clay or plaster, Husk made intricate sculptures out of food products stolen from Brooklyn supermarkets. His most accomplished piece to date was a lemon Bundt cake with cherry icing, a work he called *Satan's Hollow (Key Food, #1)*.

The enclosed bio was surprisingly thorough. Gerry had attempted suicide twice since his wife had given him the boot. He'd been busted several times for public intoxication. During that difficult time, he prowled Red Hook at night and spray-painted the words "Eat My Death" on parked cars, brick walls, and subway cars, but he refused to sign his work for fear of the persecution great artists have endured throughout history. Then: nothing. Gerry "The Balls" Husk was blocked. So he moved into a men's SRO and started doing crystal meth.

Parker, Gerry's new benefactor, was thirty-two, single, and a nightly drinker. He longed for a meaningful relationship in his life, but he always second-guessed his decisions, couldn't commit to anything for long, and in the process had made his life small. A therapist once tried to explain to Parker that he was emotionally anorexic, due to unresolved childhood traumas. Parker dealt with it by never going back to therapy.

The enclosed biography of his artist came as a welcome distraction. Gerry "The Balls" Husk eventually fought his way back from the brink of suicide. He did a stint in rehab, eighteen days, and made a strong comeback in the fall of 2009. His one-man show in the Bedford Avenue L Station garnered quite a bit of critical attention. His most remarked-upon work was a coffin-shaped Jell-O mold in which he suspended a McDonald's French fry and a razor blade. He called it *The Last Supper*.

"Jell-O's my strongest medium," he told a student reporter from Stuyvesant High School, a junior fulfilling his journalism credit. "I want to dry hump the world," the artist said.

The article ran on page three in *The Spectator* and this renewed attention to his work fueled Husk. He was back!

Parker tossed aside the pages. A Bundt cake? The Last Supper? It all seemed a little silly and forced. Dry hump the world? What did that mean? A part of him wanted to walk away from the whole enterprise, demand a refund and maybe even an apology, but hadn't he done this a thousand times before, inched closer to something challenging only to pull away again? And maybe Gerry's stuff *was* innovative. Who was Parker to question Gerry's vision?

He retrieved the bio from the floor. "You don't have a degree in art history," he said aloud. "So why are you pretending to know what's good or bad?"

As a benefactor, Parker had to put his own prejudices and ignorance aside. His adopted artist needed room to grow without outside interference from him or anyone else. But Parker couldn't stop thinking about that Bundt cake. It didn't resonate—not at first. But on the train to work he kept thinking about it. Who didn't enjoy a Bundt cake when it came right down to it? They were delicious and you could cut them so easily on account of that hole in the center. Each slice came out perfectly.

Before encountering Gerry's work, Parker had never before meditated on the *idea* of a Bundt cake. Who consumed them? The bourgeoisie. *Satan's Hollow (Key Food, #1)* provoked him to think about his own middle-class upbringing and the cakes his mother had baked. Surprisingly, he had never before considered the implications of what had been on the dining room table of his childhood home. Removed from its known context and placed in a museum, a Bundt cake invited him to interrogate his life, his untroubled politics, and his country's history.

Thanks to his minimum donation, Parker learned in the next Info-Pak, his adopted artist bought a pair of navy blue Dickies work pants, a thermal undershirt, and a bong. "Gerry is thriving, thanks to you. If you could give a little more each month, your artist will continue to make enormous strides. Only ten dollars more per month would make you a Gold Donor."

Parker checked the "yes" box and sent it back in. He was making a difference in another person's life. No amount of money could equal that feeling. Miraculous how that worked, Parker thought. You thought you were giving life to the artist but, in fact, the artist was giving birth to an unformed part of you.

Parker told everybody at the office about the adoption. "His name is Gerry," he said, beaming. He passed around a photo showing Gerry's adorable chin scruff and crow's feet, his mischievous middle finger extended.

Carla Donofrio, the Marketing Admin., stepped out from behind her desk and hugged him. "I heard you adopted a child, Parker." Then she looked at the photo. "Oh, my God," she said, flinching. "What's that?"

"That's my boy," Parker said. "That's Gerry."

Michael Bean, a junior account manager, gave him a double thumbs up, the phone cradled between his cheek and shoulder. "Talk later," he mouthed.

The next envelope he received from the Adopt Art headquarters contained three heartrending photographs of Gerry "The Balls" Husk lunging through the streets of a rapidly gentrified Red Hook, a hand-rolled smoke dangling from his lips. Dressed in a worn flannel shirt and ripped jeans, his belly distended, Parker's artist looked sick, depraved, in need of a hot shower.

"I can give you ten dollars more each month," he told the phone operator. "But that's it! Please help Gerry get what he needs."

Parker kept his coworkers apprised of his artist's growth. "He's over a hundred pounds. Three meals a day. Vegetables even. He's completely off meth. In fact, he just celebrated a ninety-day anniversary at Hugs Not Drugs."

"An anniversary every ninety days? My wife would love that," Michael Bean quipped. "That's right up her alley."

"It's not that kind of anniversary," Parker told him. "Don't belittle Gerry's achievements."

"What?"

"That's what we call emotional abuse."

"He's getting so big," Carla said, looking at the latest photos. At heart, Carla was a kind person. She felt bad, she had told him, about her initial horrified reaction. Now she had become as supportive as anyone. "Time flies," she said. "Enjoy it while you can."

On the first of every month, the Adopt Art people tapped into Parker's credit card. Each month he noticed additional charges, six to eleven bucks extra, usually for taxes and surcharges and miscellaneous fees, in addition to his added payments as a Premium Platinum Member, but it was never enough to concern him. Not at first, anyway. Gerry seemed to be enjoying his new bong. In the most recent photographs Parker noticed a fresh tattoo on his artist's neck, a dagger piercing a spider web.

"You look good, Parker," Carla said to him one day. They were alone in the conference room after a staff meeting. She appraised him from head to foot, nodding her head. "Are you working out?"

He laughed and gathered his papers. "No time for that, Carla. Not these days."

She stepped closer. "I can't stop thinking about your adopted artist. It's so weird how you sponsor him. I mean, it's cool. It's different."

"Don't even get me started." He smiled at her. "I've definitely got my hands full with Gerry, that little dickens."

She touched his forearm with her fingertips. "I'd love to hear more about it. Hey, we should get a drink sometime. What do you think?"

Normally he would have jumped at her offer. Carla was conscientious, kind, and generous, not to mention physically and intellectually attractive, but his needs had to come second to his new responsibilities as a benefactor. Maybe some people could just traipse all over town without a care in the world, but Parker was accountable now to another life.

"Sorry," he said to her. "Wish I could."

"I completely understand. Let me know if you change your mind."

At night Parker worried about his artist. He slept very little, his ear trained to the ring of his phone. Would the Adopt Art phone operator call to tell him that Gerry needed him?

One morning, exhausted from lack of sleep, Parker staggered to his local playground and sat with all the young parents and nannies. Eager to swap stories, he held a recent photo of Gerry "The Balls" Husk in his lap. They all seemed to know one another. They traded mirthful banter about sippy cups, organic snack foods, and the viscosity of feces.

"Tell me about it," Parker said and rolled his eyes. "They do make messes."

One of the mothers spoke up. "Sir, do you have a child here? At the park?"

Grateful for the opening to connect, Parker passed around his favorite photo of Gerry sunbathing at Riis Park in his banana yellow thong, a strip of zinc on his nose. Sweet Gerry had never looked happier or healthier. His neck tattoo glistened with oil.

She inspected it briefly before handing it back. "I think you should leave."

"Ma'am, the thing about being a benefactor is—"

"I will call the police."

Undeterred by the scorn, Parker carried Gerry's photograph to the tallest slide in the park. He climbed the steel rungs and pushed the curling paper down the shiny dented surface. He descended the ladder, ran around lightning quick and caught his adopted artist at the bottom of his descent.

Then Parker laid the photograph in a swing, pinned it down with a heavy rock, and pushed with all his might. The other mothers watched him, whispering to one another. He gathered the photo from the dirt, where it had fallen, and strolled out of the park, shouting, "Who wants ice cream?"

An hour later, Parker's boss called his cell and demanded to know why he wasn't at work. Was he taking a vacation day?

Parker stared out the window of Baskin-Robbins, infuriated. After his nine loyal years at the agency, never demanding a raise or a promotion, this was the thanks he got?

"I'll be in tomorrow," Parker told him in a chilly but professional tone.

"Wise choice," his boss said. "That is, if you want to keep your job."

"Watch it, Pops. You're cruising for a discrimination lawsuit."

Parker actually said this after the old man had hung up, to spare his boss the embarrassment of being on the wrong side of history.

That night, late, while Parker was watching TV alone in his living room, he caught the Adopt Art commercial again. The same two characters appeared, the gorgeous thespian and the struggling artist, Beauty and the Beast. Again Beauty encouraged viewers at home to donate to the cause. This time Parker understood—no, he felt that this auburn-haired woman, this talented young person had, of course, been a child not long ago, riding a bicycle for the first time, smiling up at a parent or guardian, experiencing all the guilt and sorrow of a human life. Perhaps she had sat beside her piano instructor on a hard bench, her back straight, her little hands perched over the keys, as Parker once had, practicing scales over and over. Perhaps she had drawn a detailed picture of a bulldog, every fold in its face precise, its sad eyes so "expressive," a drawing that Mrs. Lucas praised in front of everyone in class, announcing that there was a true talent among the student body, a proclamation that resulted in the artist getting his head dunked in a toilet by Chris Andruzzi, the toughest kid in school. This time, though, Parker ignored Beauty and focused on the Beast. The dirty artist in the Slayer shirt had once been a child, too. Perhaps he had loved bottle rockets and the sound of ambulance sirens. Perhaps he'd dreamed of being a brain surgeon or a big league shortstop, before life turned sour for him and he decided to pursue the arts.

Tears welled in Parker's eyes. He saw them both, this older man and younger woman—and the whole world, for that matter—as miraculous and fragile. How could we make such crude distinctions between people? Nobody was one thing alone, he realized, neither Beauty, nor Beast. Both sides warred within us.

The mailman brought terrible news that afternoon. Parker's adopted artist, his boy, sweet Gerry Husk, had been arrested.

According to the enclosed police report, Gerry had assaulted a coffee shop barista, a graduate student in Fordham's Theology department. Evidently Gerry tried to punch the young man in the mouth after a dispute over an insufficient amount of caramel in his macchiato. Gerry fled the scene with a full bottle of caramel syrup in hand but was later apprehended in a taqueria next door. Eleven eyewitnesses were willing to testify against him. Gerry "The Balls" Husk ruined quite a few lunches that afternoon.

The theology student was unharmed, and even finished his shift, but later claimed to have suffered a debilitating ontological wound that required weeks of bed rest. His lawyer filed a lawsuit seeking six figures in damages.

Of course Parker blamed himself. He hadn't shown enough interest in Gerry's latest projects. And he'd ignored Gerry's obvious cries for help.

Parker tried to remember if he knew any trial lawyers. He entertained fantasies of tracking down the theology student and silencing him for good.

Unable to sleep that night, Parker lay in bed questioning everything. What kind of person had he become? Was Gerry "The Balls" Husk really his type of artist? Parker had tried to like *The Last Supper* but couldn't find the beauty or deeper meaning in it. Now Gerry had brutalized somebody in broad daylight. His adopted artist had clearly violated the terms of their contract. Gerry's actions were not defensible.

After another sleepless night, Parker called the Adopt Art headquarters in Cincinnati. "I'm not sure I really *like* my artist," he told the operator. "Can you match me with somebody else, please? A nice quiet landscape painter maybe? Or a water colorist? Or maybe even a senior citizen trying to make one last splash in the crafts world before the final curtain call of death?"

"Impossible." The person on the other end sounded almost angry. "You agreed to sponsor Gerald Husk for the minimum period of eighteen years."

"Eighteen years?" Parker said, his own voice sounding foreign to him. "I thought it was only for six months, a year at the most."

"Because you didn't cancel at any time during the twenty-eight day introductory period, you committed yourself to the full contract."

He couldn't think of anything to say.

"As I'm sure you know," she continued, "the Adopt-an-Artist program is a tiered system designed to give your artist the education he or she deserved but probably didn't receive. This, of course, includes overseas travel."

Parker's mouth went dry.

"The contract is binding, sir. We have your signature and your social security number and your credit card number, of course, so we'll take care of everything. Your artist hopes to study in Rome, Paris, and Tijuana."

In a daze Parker hung up and took to his bed.

At work the following morning, Parker asked Carla to look over the agreement. She told him he was screwed. "Why on earth did you sign that thing?" she said. "Did you even read it?"

Parker shrugged. "It seemed like a good idea at the time. I was kind of lonely."

Carla wouldn't drop it. She continued to grill him. Had he just acted on a whim, drunkenly indulging himself, without considering the consequences? So many men thought they could be benefactors, she said, but few of them gave thought to the logistics.

"My life seemed kind of meaningless," he told her. "I thought this would help."

"Next time," she said, "get a puppy."

He lost a considerable amount of weight. Once a month his father called long distance to make him feel worse about himself.

Parker's father talked about the advantages of having children when one was "young enough to enjoy them." He begged his son to find greater meaning in his life, clearly misunderstanding the emotional bond shared between an artist and a benefactor.

"Gerry and I will be just fine without your interference," Parker told him. "You don't understand my generation. The art world is different now. Clement Greenberg is dead."

"Who?" his father said.

"Exactly."

"Help me to understand," his father said in a calm voice. "Tell me again, please, what this man *does*."

"He's a gelatin sculptor, Dad. A wildly talented one. You'd be amazed by how many razor blades and French fries he incorporates into his molds. He cut his teeth on baked goods, but this new medium opens the door for greater innovation."

"I see." His father's sigh sounded like a gust of wind strong enough to fell power lines. "And he calls himself Gerry the *what*?"

"Okay, sure." Parker chuckled. "Gerry's a little rough around the edges, I'll grant you that, but he's a good boy at heart. He deserves a second chance in life. We all deserve a second chance. Jesus Christ got one, didn't he?"

His father fell silent.

"And look at J.C. now," Parker continued, filling the terrible silence with words. "He ascended to Heaven and is seated at the right hand of the Father. He's seated at the Table of Righteousness." This was a wild guess but it sounded right in his head. "Supping on the Fruits of Salvation."

"Where did we go wrong with you?" his father said. "Was it something we did?"

Parker didn't respond. His mother wept in the background.

"Do you hear that?" his father said. "Do you understand what you're doing?"

Parker couldn't sleep after that. He couldn't do anything more for his artist. Nobody could. If Gerry possessed real talent, he'd transform his suffering into a work of high value. He would triumph over his own mortality by producing something fine and lasting and true. If Gerry didn't have talent or genius, well, then he could join the rest of humanity. Billions of people struggled every day to find value in their lives. Gerry would simply take his place among them. But, until then, someone had to support this boy and show him love. Was there anything more poignant and hopeful than an amateur artist who had yet to be disabused of his fantasies?

"Do it for us, Gerry," Parker said, lying on his bed, alone. "Dry hump the world." He looked up at a hairline fracture in the ceiling. "Hump it for all its worth."

I FEEL FREE

I'd been dating Karen for two weeks, maybe three, when she told me an ex-lover was stalking her. They'd broken up over a year ago, she insisted, but Trang just couldn't take a hint. He followed her everywhere, threatened her with a bowie knife, and had even kicked another man repeatedly in the mouth with his combat boots. Major reconstructive surgery. "He's huge," she said. "And crazy."

I didn't feel an immediate urge to speak. I am not a big man, and any comment from me, I believed, would only emphasize the disparity in our physiques.

"I don't want to freak you out or anything, Wayne," she said, "but Trang's probably parked across the street right now, in that donut shop parking lot, watching us with his high-powered binoculars."

I glanced at the window. "Interesting." I didn't want to appear weak or excitable. "Binoculars?" I said.

"Last night I felt him watching us have sex. When my bra came off, I could feel him cursing. He was pounding his fists against his steering wheel, vowing bloody revenge. He was scraping his knife against a small gray stone. That's how he sharpens the blade."

I laughed, still thinking it was a joke. "How could you possibly know that?"

"I just know," she said. "I know Trang."

Online dating was new to me. My friend Diamond Doug had suggested it. He said, "I know three people personally, *three*, who met their wives on the Internet."

Advice on dating from a married man always rankled me. I suspected that Diamond Doug knew he had made a terrible mistake and now wanted all his friends to do the same.

I said, "Hell no. Put my face online? 'I'm five-eleven. I like dark chocolate and literature.' No thanks."

"Listen," he said. "I'll ask one of these guys which website he used and I'll send you the link. Totally discreet. Couldn't hurt to try, right?"

I told him that I would consider it, primarily to shut him up. If I agreed, then we could talk about baseball. There were two interesting pennant races to break down and analyze.

The website, I learned the following day, was called *Get-Enmeshed.com* and dubbed itself "the online dating forum for singles who want serious commitment now!"

The exclamation point gave me pause. I ignored Doug's email for over a month, until I heard from an old friend that my ex, Mariana, was engaged to a human rights lawyer in New Orleans. The wedding was set for June. My solitude proved unbearable after that. I had eaten a thousand meals alone in the past year, mostly on park benches and street corners. My cheek bulging with lo mein, I watched couples pass hand in hand, laughing. That was no way to live. So I set up a dating profile, describing myself as "independent" and "friendly but shy."

I met Karen outside the Italian restaurant she picked in Prospect Heights. When we walked in, the hostess squealed and pulled her into a big hug. "You're looking good. No more bags under your eyes." She gave Karen's breasts a friendly squeeze. "Putting some weight back on, nice, nice." I didn't like the sounds of this. Why was this woman fondling my date's bosoms? The hostess turned to me, her eyes shining. "I know this bitch from River Glen. Hey, were you there, too? Over in the men's ward?"

I shook my head no.

"Come this way," she said and sat us by a side window.

While we perused our menus, I asked Karen about River Glen. She said it was a rehab in New Jersey. I chose not to pursue the topic.

After dinner, we took a midnight walk through Prospect Park. It was okay but not especially memorable or passionate. We kissed goodnight before she drove home to her place in Canarsie. "I'll call you," I said, but I wasn't entirely sure about that. A recovering addict was not exactly what I was looking for. But at least I had tried online dating and could tell Doug that I'd given it a shot.

The following evening Karen showed up at my apartment building with takeout Thai and a Scrabble board. Personally I believe one should always call first before showing up, but I let her in anyway. Surprisingly, we had a lot of fun that night. Karen crushed me with triple word scores. By her own admission, she had played a lot of Scrabble at River Glen. At the end of the night we kissed again, this time with a little more enthusiasm.

When we ended up in bed together I suddenly remembered why people enjoyed sex so much.

In the morning Karen helped me to decorate my one-bedroom apartment, the modest lodging in Midwood I'd retreated to after my breakup with Mariana. It was true that I hadn't done much to personalize the space since I'd moved in. I'd simply ignored its unloveliness. The thin, frayed carpet fell somewhere on the color spectrum between beige and turd brown. The walls were flat white and scuffed, unpainted during my tenancy. I had tacked up only one print, "Nude in the Tub," by my favorite painter, Pierre Bonnard, who I imagined to be a private man, somebody like me. Karen brimmed with ideas about interior decoration. She was always knocking down walls in her mind.

My apartment featured a small washer/dryer setup. When she saw them, Karen was thrilled. "Are these new?" she said. The landlord had installed them himself the previous month. He had also raised the rent a hundred bucks, but at the time it seemed like a fair deal. "These aren't even coin-op," she said, hugging me.

Karen transformed corners with low tables, spider plants, and driftwood sculptures. Bright tapestries brought the walls alive. She even added a phone line for herself. I admired her creativity and enthusiasm. Day after day she continued to add little flourishes to the place. Plastic geraniums. Candelabra. I strolled around my apartment like a tourist. On my bare white walls Karen had hung photographs of herself having fun in not-so-distant locations. One showed her at Canarsie Pier, another at the cemetery. She stood next to fishermen and tombstones, beaming. I wondered who was working the camera. The unknown photographer's shadow fell across her face, obscuring her features.

Karen was temporarily unemployed, so she did most of her interior decorating while I was at work. I'd come home at night to find another surprise waiting for me. "Isn't it exciting?" she'd ask. Or she'd say, "It'll grow on you."

On the mantel above the fake fireplace I kept a black and white portrait of my parents: a wedding photo from 1977. Karen exiled them to the bathroom. Arms around each other's shoulders, they laughed from their cold perch on the toilet tank. They watched me urinate and floss. But the mantel wasn't barren. In Mom and Dad's place stood a framed eight-by-eleven photograph of a man I'd never seen before.

"Karen, who is this?" I said, peering into the plastic frame. His ragged bangs looked like they had been trimmed with nail clippers.

Karen didn't hear my question. She was power drilling a series of holes into the ceiling so that she could hang some ferns.

"Karen," I called out in a louder voice. "Who's this dude on my mantel?"

She turned off the drill, flipped up her protective goggles, and joined me on the opposite side of the room.

"Oh, that's just Trang," she said, taking my hands in hers. She kissed me. Then she trailed her lips across my cheek to my left earlobe. "It's an old photograph," she breathed in my ear. "It's just there to remind me how awful he was."

I took a closer look at that photo. He had a scar above his lip that seemed to connect his nose to his mouth.

"Are you kidding me?" I said. "The stalker Trang?"

"He was so terrible," she said, eyeing his picture on the mantel. "Such an animal."

"Take it down," I said. After all, I didn't have any photographs of Mariana on display.

"It's cute that you're jealous, Wayne, but let's leave it up for a few days and see if it grows on you." She swiped a feather duster over the frame, hitting all four edges. "If you still don't like it, I'll take it down and you'll never see it again. Does that sound like a fair deal?"

"It sounds insane," I said.

My married buddy Diamond Doug, the reformed wild man, often talked about the compromises he needed to make with his wife Liz. Frequently he just gave in, surrendered outright, because he knew most things weren't worth the fight. "You have to choose your battles," he said. "Otherwise you'd be fighting over everything. Who's got the energy for that? Just let her have what she wants. What do you care?"

Still, I had to draw the line somewhere. "No way," I said. I took down the photograph of Trang and buried it in a drawer. It had been a test of some sort, I decided, and I felt like I had passed.

That week Karen and I made meals together in my kitchen and talked about our lives. She told me about her former addiction to cocaine, detailing where it had taken her and what she had done to recover. She considered abstinence one of her greatest achievements in life. I chopped onions on a cutting block and found myself comparing my experiences to hers, disappointed that I had never been arrested or locked up in a women's detention center.

One evening, about three weeks after she moved in, I returned from work and found damp clothes scattered all over the living room. There were mounds of moist fabric on the steaming radiator, wet jeans draped over drying racks, T-shirts clinging to the backs of wooden chairs. Soggy gray underpants drooped above every doorframe, like mistletoe in a surrealist painting. The washer and dryer were both shuddering, rocking with the weight of their loads, but I didn't recognize any of the clothes.

I waded through the humid air. Sweat beaded on my forehead. "Hey, Karen," I called out, "it's really hot in here." All the windows were steamed. "Is the heater on? What's the deal with all this laundry?"

"It *is* hot in here," said a strange man seated on my couch.

I jumped back and raised my fists. "Who are you?" I said. He stared at me without speaking. From that distance I couldn't see the scar over his lip, and he had a shorter haircut—high and tight, military style. I felt my jaw muscles tensing. "I asked you a question, man."

"I suggested she open a window." He waved his hand, indicating the futility of the request. "She wouldn't listen."

Karen came into the room carrying a sloshing pitcher of margaritas. Lime wedges seesawed in the yellow liquid like capsized boats. "Hi there, sweetie," she said. She placed the pitcher on the coffee table and rushed toward me. She rammed her tongue into my mouth. "I missed you."

I tasted Nicorette and tequila. I disengaged my mouth from hers and said, "Who's that on the couch?"

"Hmm?" She followed the angle of my pointed finger. "Oh, him? That's just Trang."

"In the flesh," he said.

"Actually he was just leaving," Karen said pointedly. "Weren't you?"

Trang shot me a big grin. "That's news to me."

He had one slender leg crossed over the other. He wasn't nearly as big as Karen had described, but his narrow face suggested a fierce and nasty intelligence. Both of his ropy-muscled arms were slung over the back of my couch. His posture vaguely suggested crucifixion. "What's up?" he said to me. "How was work? Nine to five, what a way to make a living."

Karen squeezed both my hands in hers. "Oh, now, listen, before I forget: we really need to have that old dryer looked at. Honey! Pay attention. Stop staring at Trang. What are we gonna do about the dryer?"

I wiped a rivulet of sweat off my cheek. "What's wrong with the dryer? It's brand new."

Trang said, "This is a nice little pad you have here, Warren."

"I told you his name is Wayne." Karen stamped her foot. "Can't you remember anything? *Wayne.*"

Yawning, Trang flicked a piece of lint or a stray hair off the armrest of my couch. He leaned forward and poured himself another margarita. Then he poured one for Karen. Both rims were crusted with salt. "Whatever," he said. "You say tomato, I say Warren. Let's call the whole thing off."

"Shut up," I said to him. "I'll deal with you later." I turned toward Karen. "Can you explain this to me?"

As I approached her, I felt my foot strike against something. Trang's mouth fell open. At my feet a steel briefcase lay on its side. With astonishing quickness he leapt up and stood face to face with me. "You should watch where you're going." He picked up the case and hugged it to his chest. "This is off limits to you," he said, and walked out the door. "You don't touch. No touching."

"What the hell?" I said. "What are you two up to? Is this some kind of scam?"

"Wayne, no!" She seized my hands again. "You and I are together. Trang is a distant memory. He just came over to drop off my clothes."

As crazy as it may sound, I wanted to believe her. I really had come to enjoy Karen's company. With her around I never knew what to expect. Every day promised a new dopamine spike of fear or elation. She laughed a lot and talked about things I'd never thought about before. She kept the apartment clean. She hung stuff on the walls. There was always a new development. Despite her eccentricities, Karen made the place feel more like a home.

Sometimes after sex, Karen blew gently on my skin to dry the sweat. Her long hair tickled my skin as she moved slowly down my body, cooling my chest and thighs and the bottoms of my feet with little puffs of breath. I liked that almost as much as the sex itself. No one else had ever done that before. It seemed to me such a tender, thoughtful act of affection. Even Trang's presence didn't sour me. On the contrary, I found myself even more attracted to Karen, knowing that another man was still in the picture. Her smile seemed brighter, her eyes more luminous. I felt the buzz that comes from competition.

"I'll give you the benefit of the doubt," I told her. "I was just surprised, that's all. I mean, put yourself in my shoes."

"I can't even imagine," she said.

After Trang's departure, I retreated to the bedroom, where I resumed reading my Tolstoy biography. At least a week had passed since I'd last looked at it. Before I could read an entire page, Karen barged in and sat on the bed's edge. "What's the matter, Wayne? Are you depressed?"

"No, it's just . . . well. Trang," I said, my eyes still focused on the page. "I think you're still in love with him."

"You're adorable!" She kissed my cheek. "Are you jealous?"

"I'm not going to be a watchdog in my own house. I don't have the energy for that. If you're going to screw around behind my back—"

"You'll never see him again. He's history." She eyed the cover of my book. "*The Russian Master: Leo Tolstoy*. Did you ever read any Larry McMurtry? You should check out McMurtry if you're so into Tolstoy." She slid even closer to me, sucking her cough lozenge. "That McMurtry. Boy, he's something else. What a way with words. Nobody can describe a cactus like McMurtry."

I shut the book on my index finger to save my place. At the time I didn't know why I liked Karen so much. Maybe it was something in her eyes, the trusting and childlike quality in them. Just beneath Karen's coarse surface—the oval scar on her back from an ex-boyfriend's cigarette, the tribal tattoos on her upper arms—there was a sweet girl who had trusted the wrong people along the way. She certainly didn't need a guy like Trang in her life, a man who couldn't recognize her true nature. She needed a more empathetic partner, somebody like me.

"McMurtry's good?" I asked her.

She waved the question away. "Just read him. You'll see. You'll see what I mean about old McMurtry."

After a moment of charged silence, Karen stood up and left the room. She shut the door quietly behind her.

For the next hour I read about Leo Tolstoy's dramatic experiences in the Caucasus. He fought bloody skirmishes with mountain tribesmen. He went days without eating. He was a rugged, intelligent man who would change the course of world literature. I immersed myself in his story, trying to gain strength and guidance from it.

My bedroom door swung open again. "Knock knock, Lonesome Dove," Karen said. She carried a stack of clean clothes into the room.

Humming a song under her breath, Karen yanked open dresser drawers and slammed them shut. "We—are—family," she sang, wagging her head. "I got all my sisters and me."

"Karen, please," I said, not looking up from my book. "I'm trying to read."

She approached the bed, sat down, and took a long look at the book's cover. "You think Sir Leo Tolstoy liked to shampoo that big beard of his?"

I sighed. "I don't know how Tolstoy behaved in the bathtub. And for the record, Tolstoy was a count, not a knight."

My tone was more acerbic than I'd intended. But Karen didn't seem to notice. She leaned closer to inspect the book's cover. She tipped it back with her hand, preventing me from reading it. "What a beard, huh?"

I smelled her peach shampoo. "Karen," I said.

She stroked the image of Tolstoy's beard with her forefinger. "He looks crazy," she said. "And I've seen some kooks, boy. He fits the profile."

I looked down at the photograph or daguerreotype or whatever it was. He was in his most pious religious phase then, an old man wearing some kind of white gown and seeker's sandals.

I said, "He was obsessed with God and vegetarianism and humility when that was taken."

"Yeah, I bet he was," Karen said, "but you know he spent some quality time on that beard each morning. Probably used a top-notch conditioner and some French oils, too. Scrubbed it up good." She paused. "But you know Trang's the same way. Some nights he'll spend a couple hours polishing up those snow globes he carries around. He really takes his time with it."

"Snow globes," I said.

"He's pretty intense about it."

Karen walked out of the room humming. I couldn't even enjoy my damn book after that. No matter what the biographer wrote about the Russian master's selflessness and his boundless humanity, I imagined Tolstoy lathering his beard with imported French or Italian conditioner, smiling at his face in the mirror, while behind him Trang held a snow globe up to the light and dabbed at it with a cloth.

The following evening, during dinner, Karen informed me that Trang was on his way. "He wants to apologize for inconveniencing you," she said.

"Couldn't he call or send a text?" I said.

As if on cue, Trang walked in without knocking. "Hey, gang," he said. I noticed he was holding a red Netflix envelope. "Oh this?" he said. "It's a classic." In his other hand he carried the snow globe case.

Karen explained in a loud whisper that the DVD was a peace offering. She said that it was very difficult for Trang to be friendly with other men. He was making a concerted effort.

I sighed. "What's the movie called?"

"Okay, Curious George, I'll give you a hint," Trang said. "The cast includes such luminaries as Dudley Moore, Liza Minnelli, and Sir John Gielgud. Does that ring a bell?"

"No," I said.

My couch seated only two people comfortably—it was more of a loveseat—and we had a hard time deciding who should sit where. After a brief negotiation, Karen decided to get down on the floor, which left Trang and me side by side on the loveseat.

"Cozy, no?" he said.

I moved my knee away from his.

"This is the greatest movie ever made," Trang announced. "Get ready to have your dangler knocked off."

Early into the screening Trang took out his bowie knife and began to sharpen it on his stone. The scraping sound chilled my blood. He kept looking over at me and popping his eyebrows up and down.

It was a decent comedy, but hardly the best ever. Trang and Karen howled with laughter. They delivered lines in unison with the actors, warned me to get ready before funny scenes, and slapped high fives throughout. Afterward, Trang called it a brilliant socioeconomic parable, an allegory of man's inhumanity to man. He walked out the door, still chuckling to himself.

"Karen, we need to talk," I said later that night. We sat side by side on the loveseat that Trang had just vacated. "This doesn't seem to be working out. I think we should break up."

Karen buried her face in her hands, refusing to look at me. "And I've been so happy," she said. "Please. Don't do this. Don't end this." Her shoulders sagged. "Let's just see where it takes us."

"You've been happy?" I said, surprised.

"I'm in love." She looked at me through the spaces between her fingers. "Can't you see that?"

Alone in the bedroom, I thought about our relationship. What kind of future did we have together? I weighed the pros and cons. There was companionship, clean laundry, and Trang. Was it an ideal situation? No. I wouldn't say that. But you had to expect a certain amount of discomfort when you shared your life with another person. Hell, I was no prize myself. I knew that. And if I wanted a romantic relationship to succeed, my buddy Doug kept reminding me, then I needed to understand the logistics of surrender and sacrifice. Nothing good came without a struggle.

I decided to stick it out for another week.

"Can I offer you piece of advice?" Trang said four days later. He was seated at the kitchen table, drinking coffee. He had the real estate section of *The New York Times* spread before him. When I didn't reply, he forged ahead anyway. "You're a pussy," he said.

"What?" I said and cinched the knot of my plaid flannel bathrobe. "Stand up. Say that again."

I'd been in scraps before. In high school I fought at least once a week, surrounded by a ring of leering bitter faces, knowing the up-front cruelty of kids, and there was a period in my life when I began to look forward to the afternoon's final bell. Even though I hadn't chosen this identity for myself, I had become a brawler. At 3:30, I stood in the center of the circle with a bloody lip, refusing to go down. A perfectly landed punch to the jaw would end it. I loved that feeling. Somebody was definitely going to lose. The best thing ever was when a bigger guy charged at you, growling threats and curses, and you smoothly turned his own momentum against him. I had brought my right knee down on more than one blood-spurting nose. I had elbowed people, hard, in their kidneys. I'd also been choked out and made to eat dirt.

"I'll throw down right now," I said to Trang. Even though it had been almost a decade since I'd last landed a punch, I warmed instantly to the idea. "Stand up. Let's have some fun."

"Holy cow." He smiled. "Don't shoot the messenger, guy."

At that moment I wanted to grab Trang by the shoulders and throw him out the door. I wanted to smash his face in with my fist. But I remembered what Karen had said about reconstructive surgery, and about how Trang had once kicked a man in the mouth, repeatedly. I wondered if a confrontation was worth it. I took another look at that bowie knife sheathed on his belt.

"Let's examine your relationship with Karen," he said. "You're playing this thing all wrong, my friend. I'm just trying to help you here."

"I don't need your help."

"Women," he said, "want to believe that we—men—are much more unpredictable and dangerous than we really are." He lowered his voice. "Usually I try not to disavow them of this misconception, if you know what I mean."

I felt tired, lightheaded. "What are you talking about?" I sat down across from him.

"Beat your chest a little, Warren. You're too nice and she'll walk all over you." He leaned forward on his elbows. "They're like little rabbits. Sometimes you gotta jack up their heartbeats. Make them think their life is in jeopardy, and then you rush in and save the day. They're so relieved, so aroused, they forget you put them in peril in the first place."

I rose to my feet and put my mug in the sink. "You don't deserve Karen," I said and walked out of the kitchen.

Later that night, when I returned home from work, I found the living room windows all steamed up again.

"I made baked ziti," Trang said and emerged from the kitchen carrying a steaming casserole dish. He wore an apron that read COOKIN' WITH GAS. His bowie knife was strapped, as always, to his hip. "Get it while it's hot, kiddos. Mama's famous red sauce."

I joined Karen by the washer/dryer combo. She was frantically adding figures on a small notepad. "Yes, sir. Have it for you by tomorrow," she said into the phone. "That's thirteen-fifty, total. Okay. Yes. Bye." She hung up. "Hi, hon." She stepped forward for a kiss. "How was work?"

Before I could reply, the phone rang again. She flipped her hair to the side and lifted the phone to her ear. "Karen's Anytime Laundry. This is Karen speaking."

"Hey," I said. "We need to have a serious talk."

"Watch your foot."

I looked down. My toes had grazed Trang's steel briefcase. "Jesus," I said. "Why doesn't he store that in a safer place?"

After dinner, I overheard Trang talking long distance to a snow globe collector out in Vancouver. He described the delicate hand-blown glass of his collectibles. He talked about the subpar quality of the glitter in the newer models—shaved porcelain and bone chips had, of course, been the industry standard for decades—and he reminded the man that distilled water, which could be found in the best globes, did not turn yellow or leave any residue on the inside of the glass.

I still had a hard time believing that he was serious.

Soon Trang was shouting, pacing in the living room. Enraged, he gesticulated with his free hand and called the man an ignoramus, a world-class shithead. The snow globes from Graceland and Alcatraz were from his dead grandmother's private collection; he wouldn't let them go for cheap. They were exceedingly rare. "Go look them up in the red book," he said. "Stop wasting my time, you clown."

An hour later I learned that Trang had invited some folks over. Strangers passed through the living room with their hands buried in potato chip bags. Others arrived and peered into the fridge. Were they friends of Karen, too? I couldn't keep up. They seemed to know where to find everything: the various soups and spaghettis; the paper plates and plastic ware; the remote control.

An elderly woman with a small dog in her arms exited my bathroom and informed me that we needed more toilet paper.

Shaken, I called my former ally, Diamond Doug, even though I knew he couldn't hang out with me anymore. He had a child on the way. Long gone were the days when the two of us could just spontaneously head off to the bar together, throw darts all night or watch *SportsCenter* on the TV suspended above the bar.

I began to tell Doug about my bizarre houseguest but he interrupted me and launched into a story of his own. His in-laws were visiting from Illinois. They were outrageously tall Midwesterners who stayed for stretches of up to ten days at a time. They slept on the pullout couch, ate all his food, complimented him and smiled incessantly.

"It makes my life a living hell," he said. "Consider yourself lucky, bro."

"It's way worse over here."

"You'll get used to it," he said.

"There's this crazy guy named Trang who's always—"

"Dude, I've heard all this from you before. 'Her ankles are too thick.' Or: 'She doesn't read enough books.' You want to be alone forever? That's cool. Be alone. You'll be another Saint Francis of Assisi tossing seeds to all the birds."

"This one is different. She—"

"Nothing surprises me anymore. I have seen it all. Trust me on this one. *What?*" Now he was talking to his wife in the background. "No, it's not Frannie. It's Wayne. Okay, okay. *Okay.*"

"Doug," I said, my voice cracking. "I need help."

"Gotta go. Liz is waiting for a phone call. We're sharing my phone because hers—Long story. Anyway, hang in there."

Trang flipped through a nylon case of my old CDs and pulled out *The Very Best of Cream.* He played it at full volume. His favorite track evidently was "I Feel Free." He stood at the stereo and pressed repeat each time it ended. There was a time when I had really enjoyed that album, too. Jack Bruce had a wonderful singing voice. But my musical tastes had changed radically in the eighteen years since I'd first purchased the CD. In fact, I didn't even listen to CDs anymore. Hearing the same Cream tune over and over was an insidious form of torture.

"Slowhand," Trang said, bobbing his head. We were home alone together on a Friday night. Karen was out returning clothes to her many customers around the city. "Slowhand was in this band."

I averted my eyes from an air guitar solo and took out my meditation journal. I still hoped that one day I, like Tolstoy, would write something beautiful, something profound and illuminating about human nature. With a tiny pencil I scribbled: Trang likes Cream.

I sat there staring at my words.

Trang stood next to one of the speakers, cocked his head to the side, and pressed his ear to the woofer. "Cream was a power trio. Bass, drums, guitar. Man, those suckers rocked the sixties into oblivion. Case closed."

I shut my journal. "Where are you from, Trang?"

"What?"

"Where. Are. You. From?" I shouted.

"Canada," he hollered back.

"How long have you been in New York?"

"Feels like forever." He was getting ready to press Repeat.

"You were born in Canada?"

"Not exactly." He turned up the volume.

We said nothing after that. I listened to "I Feel Free" four more times, then I retreated to the bedroom, shut the door behind me, and inserted foam ear plugs into my head.

Toward the end of his life, Tolstoy moved away from his beloved Yasnaya Polyana, his sprawling family estate, to live an ascetic life in a monastery. He renounced his birthright as a member of the aristocracy. "I will live simply," he proclaimed. "Without resources. God will guide me." Ten days later, he died of heart failure in a railroad station in Astapovo. A porter found him dead on a rickety cot. "He looked just like any other corpse," the porter said to a journalist. "Sort of desiccated, like an old pear. We get corpses here all the time. At the time I didn't know he was Lev Tolstoy, God rest his soul."

An hour later, when I came out of the bedroom for a snack, I found Trang standing on my loveseat holding a hairbrush to his lips. The stereo was cranked as high as it could go. Even with the foam plugs jammed into my ears, I felt Jack Bruce's voice thumping on my sternum like a fist.

I stood in the doorway and watched. Karen emerged from the bathroom still wearing her slick yellow raincoat, her hair in a ponytail. She emptied her pockets on the coffee table, spilling out clumps of wet bills. She looked beautiful and flushed from the exertion of carrying hundreds of pounds of laundry around Brooklyn. Her forehead and cheeks were wet with rain.

Trang swayed his hips from side to side, the hairbrush clutched in both hands. He lip-synched lyrics about two lovers who move like the sea and therefore feel free.

A smile bloomed on Karen's face, spreading from her mouth to her eyes. She stripped off her soaked raincoat and flung it on the floor.

Trang serenaded her, his eyes clamped shut, the hairbrush now gripped in his left fist. His right hand was pressed, fingers splayed, against his chest. It was a moving display.

Karen looked at Trang as she had never once looked at me. She smoothed a few wet curls back from her forehead and watched him with intense focus. Trang turned his body fully toward her and made a circular motion with his hips.

I kept the earplugs in. I didn't even need to watch his lips to know what he was singing. I knew the lyrics by heart.

Trang, still standing on my couch, smiled down at her and let her know, through the medium of Cream, that she was the sun shining on him and because of that he felt free.

When the song was over, Karen laughed and blew kisses at him.

It was a humid night, the streets still slick from an earlier rain. Karen and Trang sat out on the stoop, drinking malt liquor from forty-ounce bottles. He'd dragged the stereo over to the sill, so that they could listen to his song from outside. I think he also had the remote control because the song kept repeating when it ended.

I thought about calling Mariana, my ex in New Orleans. I practiced the message I would leave if I reached her voicemail. "Oh, hey there, Riana. Wayne here. Just hanging out in Brooklyn, enjoying a night in with my amazing new girlfriend. Hope you're doing well." But I decided against it. Mariana was probably busy with wedding preparations.

It was time for dinner anyway. The kitchen light, I noticed, had been left on again. Nobody appeared too concerned about my electric bills.

There was no ham, cheese, or tuna in the kitchen. No bread or mayo. Karen hadn't gone shopping in over a week. The vodka and gin bottles were both empty. The music pounded out into the street, the speakers facing the open window.

On the breakfast table was the steel briefcase, its lid open. I stepped closer and looked. Inside were eight pristine glass orbs, each one snug inside its purple foam cut out. The case alone was worth a grand or two, Trang had once claimed. He took great pleasure in detailing the history behind its acquisition. He'd spotted it in a Niagara Falls pawnshop. The proprietor had no idea what he held in his possession. Trang paid him fifty bucks and laughed all the way to the casino. According to Trang, the steel briefcase had once been owned by Umberto Granaglia, the world famous Bocce master. Oval scoops in the purple foam interior once held the superstitious Granaglia's lucky balls; now they cradled Trang's vintage collectibles.

I bent over the case. A yellow tack cloth was folded lengthwise and rested on a Paris Art Deco globe. I pulled out one of the prettiest ones—a pre-fire Cocoanut Grove, circa 1941—and inspected it closely, turning it under the light. I shook it, flipped it upside down. The more I looked at it, the better I understood. I understood why he loved it so.

I smashed it on the kitchen floor. The glass shattered so beautifully. Distilled water dribbled out. Silently I stared down at this mess at my feet. I felt guilty for about a second or two. Then I pulled out each of the remaining seven globes and repeated the process again and again. Giggling, I lifted my arm over my head and heaved one down on the peeling linoleum. "Oops," I said. I chucked one at the spice rack and another against the ugly wallpaper. I felt exalted. It was an orgy of demolition. God must feel like this every day, I thought, striking down innocent people and animals, destroying entire villages.

A few of the spheres—Plexiglas ones—would not break. They bounced and skidded into the baseboards. No matter how many times I struck them down they remained intact. So I had to shatter them with a rolling pin.

Only the RMS *Lusitania*, the oldest globe in the collection, remained. I captured it and swept the empty briefcase off the table. My face was damp with sweat. I walked over to the window and stopped the CD. No more Slowhand.

I finger rolled the last remaining globe over the sill and heard it shatter between them on the stoop.

"Trang," I called out, standing serenely by the crime scene. "I think I dropped something of yours. Better come look."

The front door banged open. I listened to the drumbeat of approaching footsteps. Karen preceded him into the room. "Oh my God," she said, staring wide-eyed at the floor. "What have you done?"

Trang followed. He gawked at the wreckage, his hands snapping into fists.

"My God." Karen looked up at me with pity and tenderness. "Wayne," she said. "Are you crazy, honey?" She took a step toward me. "This is so bad. He's going to kill you."

Grinning, I leaned back against the counter, and waited. Goose bumps pebbled my forearms.

Something had to happen soon. Everyone in the house could feel it.

FAMILY ALBUM

My father runs naked through the underbrush. We can hear him grunting and yelping as the brambles slap his bare skin. We are gaining on him, following the trail of blood, but we're leery. A wounded father is a dangerous creature. And canny. He may be luring us into an ambush. We would gladly beat in his brains out in the open, under the hoary night sky, but nobody is foolish enough to—

—roar at a joke he's just told at the dinner table. He repeats the punch line, as if we hadn't heard it the first time. "That's good," he says, twirling angel hair on the tines of his fork. He's drinking booze again. The ice cubes clinking in his lowball glass sound like teeth falling from a cartoon character's mouth, and you turn to him and say—

—his gentility has ossified into fear. He is nervous, that's all, which you have misconstrued as anger. You have never understood him. But you want him to know that despite all the differences of opinion, all the arguments, you love him and—

—he's struggling under the weight of the couch you're both carrying down the stairs. "Pick up your end, goddammit," he says. "Jesus Christ." His face is flushed, an artery pulsing in his forehead. Your end of the couch is not the problem. "Should we take a break?" you ask him. He glares at you over the flowery armrest. "Nonsense, boy. I've been moving furniture since you—"

—haven't said a word in ten minutes. You don't feel like talking any more. The kiddie psychologist, a skinny-armed whisperer in a beige turtleneck, plays bumper pool with you in his office on Tuesdays and Thursdays. Courts you with cold Sprites. Probes for Insights and True Feelings. He sincerely wants to know how your mother's death has affected you, and you shrug and can't even remember the last time you—

—are crying in the garage loft, after school, punching the splintered wooden crossbeam with abraded knuckles, and your father stands below, hands on hips, racking his brains for something comforting to say. "I know how you feel," he says at last. "I miss her too, boy, but it will get better, and you can't keep—"

—pulling your pants down in class to show Kristen Thomas your penis. You are the most disruptive third grader in the class. Mrs. Hendricks has her back to the students, she's scrawling multiplication problems on the blackboard, and Kristen raises her hand, saying, "Mrs. Hendricks, Mrs. Hendricks," and—

—hairy-legged men are loitering in the driveway, drinking keg beer from red plastic cups. Your father, sunburned and jovial in sunglasses, likes his team's chances in the upcoming season. "That's a solid defense," he says. "Great linebackers. Best in football." You wrap your chubby arms around his legs and he gently pushes you away. "You're too old for that now," he says. "Men shake hands with other men." He squeezes your little hand. "Good, that's a good strong—"

—bag of marijuana. Grudgingly, your father slips it into his pocket. He had been called away from work again to deal with his delinquent son. The middle school principal, Mr. Markbright, returns to the office. "He had nothing in his pockets," your father lies for you. "My son is innocent of all charges." On the drive home, he glares out the windshield, silent. At last, he turns to you and says—

—no matter how many times you end up in detention, you continue to fight after school with Luis and Eric and Glenn. Nothing personal. You've all got the energy and the time. Sometimes you pretend you're a TV wrestler who has metal chairs smashed over his head with regularity, and you fall backward into a pile of leaves, pretending to be knocked out cold, and Glenn picks up a twig and rams it into Luis's left ear, a harmless act you've seen performed countless times on TV. Luis doesn't cry or scream at first, but—

—you hear the shrill buzzing of a tattoo needle. Through heavy-lidded eyes you look down at the ugly tattoo forming on your left biceps: a flaming orange crucifix, the word ROUGHOUSIN' scrawled in arterial red ink below it, and you manage to slur, "That's ridiculous," before—

—being accepted into an art school in Brooklyn. Alone in the cramped cell of a Fort Greene studio, you smoke meth several times a day—first with a classmate, then alone—until you set your bed and carpet and clothes on fire. You flee the scene and are arrested on DeKalb Avenue and, due to the extremity of your reaction—the biting and kicking, mostly—you are court ordered to Hurley House, an inpatient rehab in Queens. Your confused father drives down to visit you, his own breath betraying him. He still believes that Listerine, a mouthwash that is thirty percent alcohol, will cover the telltale stench each morning. He brings you books, magazines, warm socks, and candy. "I see someone raking the leaves outside," you tell him, using those dull old words that can't ever express that—

—you've met someone here at the rehab, Danielle, a fellow tweaker, a stringy-haired beauty with hollowed cheeks, her dull blue eyes set deep in their sockets as though having receded from what they saw in the mirror, her pockmarked arms sinewy-thin but still giving an impression of dangerous strength, like electrical wires encased in flexible tubing, and it will it will it will be different this time, for both of you, because—

—you bring home from preschool a clay impression of your right hand, each finger painted a different color of the rainbow. A looped string emerges from the tip of the yellow middle finger, so that some adoring adult can hang it on a wall. "I made this in school," you announce with the pride of belonging, the word "school" still pregnant with a magic and exotic quality. "We did the kiln, Mommy. The kiln is hot, and Mrs. Lucas said—"

—it makes you want to die when the cold wind rattles the window, late October, and you see a resident of Hurley House, a kid your age, raking leaves on the front lawn, his movements in slow motion. He seems to know things about life that you don't. He seems to know—

—"Hey, boy," your father says, waking you from a sitting dream, "why did you set your room on fire?" He says he wants to understand. He wants to help you. "Doctor Rosman says you're a young man with great potential." His cloud-heavy face is scrubbed and tired. He's deep inside his old man's body looking out at you, and you can't imagine how to rescue him. "Dad." Your voice sounds rusty and damaged, incapable of forming the words. "Don't worry." You know him so well. He eats cold pizza for supper and reads espionage novels in bed. His wife died inelegantly many years ago. Now he still lives alone in a big house—

—"Take it outside now," she says, frying eggs in a pan for dinner. "Play with it in the yard." She takes another sip of chardonnay, the wine glass always within reach. Confused, you look down at your art project. "It's a hand," you say in your high-pitched voice. "It's my own hand. Don't you want to see—"

—Danielle perform some private ritual that you are permitted to observe: peeling a clementine with her painted thumbnail, or tweezing the little hairs on her calves or on her breast, her naked legs folded beneath her in a sunlit armchair. You love it when she bends forward, fresh from a shower, and brushes her long wet hair from the base of her neck over her scalp and down into the air before her closed eyes, a holy moment, her naked ass gleaming, the towel cast aside on the tile floor, before throwing her hair back with a luxurious slap, and—

—your father sits you down on the hospital bed and combs your long, greasy hair. "We need to do something," he says, his voice rich with American resolve. "This is not right, boy. You don't belong here." And it's impossible to explain to him that—

—nothing is more beautiful than Danielle when she sprays perfume in the air and hurries through its fragrant cloud, insuring that she smells clean and fresh but doesn't give off the stench of a thousand dead flowers, because her mother "practically showered in attar of roses," and the smell, she said, made her want to use. You've been ready to go to the group meeting for ten minutes, fifteen, thinking let's go, come on, let's go, believing that you have a right to be annoyed with her, as if she's your property now, unwilling to leave her side where it's safe and go on your own, but she's still getting dressed and she doesn't understand why you—

—would rather hide in your room, reading books all night, than go to the Sober Dance. Safe from the confusion of dealing with damaged people, in whom you see a reflection of yourself, you can sit on your bed and travel through London, Mumbai, Tokyo, and Moscow. At times you stop and savor an arresting image, your index finger marking your place in the closed book, while you stare at the glowing streetlights outside the window, ignoring—

—that you can smell your father's breath as if it were your own. Wake up now. Come back. You're safe. It's just the two of us here, sharing our genes. Dad de-clots your hair with an Ace comb. This is how the birds do it, you think but don't say. You flick a speck of lint off his sleeve. He drove all the way down from upstate, buzzed behind the wheel, to sit here in a room that you share with three other men. "Be good, okay?" he says before he leaves. "You'll be out of here soon enough." After he's gone, you move to the window and watch that same kid dragging raked-up leaves in a blue tarp, an orange knit cap on his head, and you practice what you'll say the next time Dad visits you. "Remember when we did Adventure Guides? Remember the car we made in the basement out of balsa wood and dowels?" I don't blame you for anything. "Our car lost every race."

A LOVE LETTER

Here's what I know: life is short and life is long. Allow me to explain.

In the sense that life is short, I should tell you right now, before it's too late: I love you. Crazy because in many ways you're not my ideal—not even close—and I couldn't care less. What you have is much greater than my mind could ever conceive. You've got what my grandma calls "pizazz."

But life is long, too, and no sudden changes need to be made yet. We must remain strong, angel. This might seem shocking coming from a thirteen-year-old, but I assure you I have given this ample thought. I understand all the obstacles. You're married for one thing, and if I remember correctly you have two daughters, Kelly and Kim (?), and a son named Jake in the military. And I have not yet embarked on my high school career.

In the coming four years I will have quite a bit of homework to do, not to mention chores, and my mother has imposed upon me a strict ten o'clock curfew. Believe me, I have tried to sway her with all my considerable powers of charm and rhetoric. She is a rock, unmovable. "Give it a rest, buster," she says. "You better be in by ten or no TV." It is an effective hardline position.

The good news is you work afternoons, a choice two-to-five shift, and have I failed to mention how fetching you look in that reflective vest? I rarely, if ever, think of you as a "crossing guard." You move like a dancer. You blow your whistle like one of the jazz greats we listened to and appreciated in Music Appreciation class.

True, I am impulsive, and some say it is this quality that makes me charming, but I am also patient and caring. I need you to know that I care about you. Your husband is an aloof man with a tragic sense of fashion and a hurried air, but in him I recognize a worthy foe. He will not let you go without a struggle. He climbs in and out of his minivan with the nimble prowess of a linebacker, one who can both rush the passer and cover a halfback in the flat. And yet I cannot arrest my true feelings, lock them up in that dank prison called "repression," and dump them overboard while nobody's looking on the Staten Island ferry, like so much illegal medical waste. Maybe I'm not being clear.

Lover, I understand the logistics of compromise. If, for now, we must share only eleven seconds together each day, as you shepherd me across the street, then so be it. We have had that time, and for that I should be grateful. If I were never to see you again, I would cherish the memory of our encounter yesterday, the way you spread your arms protectively, shielding me from oncoming traffic, as I bent once again over my untied lace. I have a confession: I loosened my laces beforehand, on Carroll Street, to have a few more seconds with you.

Yesterday, when I looked up at you, the sun hovered over your shoulder, illuminating your dark hair, and exposed the silhouette of your neck. I fumbled with my shoelace. At that moment my hands were like lobster claws—not in shape, of course, or even color for that matter, but in their usefulness. They were useless! And when you said, "Hurry up, for Christ's sake. What's your problem, kid?" I nearly wept with joy. I knew, then, and forevermore, that I adored you.

"Ever heard of Velcro?" you said with a laugh, and to me it was a line of poetry more arresting than anything we read this term in pre-AP English.

Ever heard of Velcro?

Éver / héard of / Vélcro?

At night, alone in my bed, I wonder: Are you chaperoning me across the street? Or am I taking you to the other side? What would your life be like without me? I don't want to say that it would be empty and meaningless and full of drudgery, because I know that you are bright and energetic. You probably have no shortage of interests. Maybe you're a talented street photographer who exhibits her work under a pseudonym to protect impressionable loved ones from controversy. Maybe you are an activist who stands outside City Hall on Saturday afternoons with your comrades, shouting about vivisection and waving gruesome placards. Maybe you're an idler, a civilized loafer, a connoisseur of repose, sprawled on the sofa in your sweats. It's even possible that you like to smoke a little hashish (am I getting warmer?) and after a hot bubble bath, you walk around the house burning things, sage, incense, and various aromatic candles. Your personal life, I admit, is none of my business. But remember these words. I am here now. And I can only cross the street with you so many times. One day I will have to keep walking and won't see you again. But when that time comes, I promise to stop at the next corner. I will turn and wave. "Thank you," I will say. "I am safe. Are you?"

You will not hear me say these words, of course, because I'll be like three hundred feet away, at least, and I'll probably only mouth the words anyway, because it would be lame to say them aloud and my cool high school friends would totally mock me, but know that I have said and meant them. Remember me, angel. To you, I was probably one of hundreds, maybe thousands, just another face passing by your corner. But you are my only one.

PUNISHMENT

Punishment is a sort of medicine.

—ARISTOTLE, *Nicomachean Ethics*

Dunston was chopping onions for dinner when "Mustang Sally" came up in his shuffle. He started thinking about his ex again, and the knife slipped. The blade bit into his skin. Bright blood dribbled down his finger, down the grooves of his palm, and seeped into the cutting block. He held his hand under the light and inspected the wound.

Later that night, he completed some chores around the house. He washed and dried dishes, vacuumed his hardwood floor, and cleared the stack of partially read books from his bed. Then he threw on his winter coat and headed outside.

In the garage he pulled the cord on his new snowblower and let it run for a while. After a quiet moment of reflection, he lowered his left hand into the spinning blades. Three fingers were sheared clean off. He laughed. Blood spattered his shoes.

"Take that, Sally," he said.

Ten minutes later, he came to on the living room floor. He felt more than heard the ringing doorbell. But after some doing, he staggered to his feet. The front door seemed jammed. He gave it a tremendous yank and greeted his visitor with a full display of clenched teeth.

"Hey, Mister D, I'm selling candy to raise money for our team uniforms," said a neighborhood kid that Dunston had always liked. "You like peanut M&Ms or the regular kind?"

Dunston, woozy from blood loss, fumbled with his wallet and managed to extricate a ten-dollar bill with his good hand. "Take it, take it," he said.

The kid stared at the expanding patch of moisture on the Dunston's gray sweatpants pocket, where his injury was concealed.

"It's all right," Dunston said. "It's only V-8 juice."

The kid backed away slowly before he turned and ran.

Dunston shut the door.

The emergency room was unavoidable. It occurred to him that Sally might hear about his injury, which would cause her to worry, so he called four of her closest girlfriends from the hospital waiting room and made them all promise not to tell her. Somehow, in all the excitement, he let slip the hospital's address, the attending physician's name, and the best free parking locations in the neighborhood. Sally, much to his relief, did not burst through the door that night, crying, in her peach sweater with the pale blue polka dots. That would have only caused a scene.

Dunston liked to write his to-do lists at night, just before bed-time, but surgery and post-op care interrupted this routine. When he got home from the hospital, he poured himself a glass of milk and wrote: "Buy milk. Pay bills. Sever arm. Water fern."

Around noon the next day, humming quietly to himself, Dunston found his hacksaw in the garage. He rolled up his sleeve and laid his arm across a sawhorse.

"I'm sorry to do this to you, Sally, but you've forced my hand."

His severed limb fell to the garage floor with a thud.

"Your loss," he whispered.

That was one man's arm that Sally Greene would never feel holding her again.

Dunston emerged from another blackout on his living room floor, his open wound geysering blood on the couch and walls. He lost approximately six quarts of blood. Nobody called or stopped by. Clearly Sally's girlfriends had kept mum on the issue, as he had requested. He checked his voicemail just to be sure, wiping blood from his eyes and peering at his blurred phone.

At three o'clock, he died.

"That'll teach her," he thought as they zipped the bag around his corpse, and he imagined hammering a railroad spike through his groin, but he was already dead and could only fantasize.

QUAGMIRE

Paige and I lay naked in bed together. Pinned beneath her, I stared at the ceiling. "Mike's great, isn't he?" I said.

"I guess," she said. "Sure. He's all right."

"That dude makes a ton of money. Way more than me. I bet he's a multi-millionaire."

"You make plenty, babe," she said.

"Not as much as Mike, though. He's making real money."

"What's real money?" She nuzzled against me, pressed her nose into my neck. "All that matters is if you're happy or not."

"Mike's fucking loaded," I said.

The following morning, I said, "Maybe we should have Mike over for dinner. What do you think?"

Paige sliced a banana over her corn flakes. "We have nothing in the fridge."

"That's cool. I'll cook."

She laughed and poured almond milk in the bowl. "You don't cook."

Phone in hand, I scrolled through my contacts looking for Mike's number. "I'll make my famous chicken in cream sauce. With the basil and sun-dried tomatoes."

"Who *are* you?" She laughed again. "You've never made that before."

"Is tomorrow good for you?"

"Declan, we have to make some decisions—tonight—about the guest list. You haven't even looked at the binder yet."

"I'll text Mike," I said. "I'll see if tomorrow works for him. But that guy's so busy—you never know. He might be in Italy or Mozambique or some place like that."

"There he is," I said at the door. "Michael Angelo, Michael Jackson. Come on in. Let me take your distressed leather jacket. Wait, is that your BMW parked outside? Paige, check out Mike's ride. Mike, you remember Paige."

"For you." Mike handed her a bottle of pinot noir.

"Wow, that's so sweet," Paige said. "You didn't have to bring anything, Mike."

"But that's what a true gentleman does," I said and threw a fraternal arm around Mike's shoulders. "This guy's got old-world charm." I gave him a playful shove. "So how's it going, Mike? What's new? Give us the goods."

"Eh." He looked at his shoes, his hands buried in his pockets. "Same old same old."

Paige and I smiled and nodded, waiting for our honored dinner guest to say more.

"Gaza." He frowned. "Am I right? If it's not one thing, it's another."

Mike, I noted, needed help with his banter. I pried the wine bottle from my fiancée's grip and headed for the kitchen. "You two get comfy on the couch," I said. "I'll just be in here makin' the chow."

In the kitchen, I pressed my ear to the door and eavesdropped on their conversation.

"Nice place," Mike said.

"We moved here after graduation. Put a lot of work into it. The floors, the woodwork. You see the exposed brick? Declan did all of that."

"Looks great now," Mike said, piling on.

"Declan's pretty handy," she said. "He does all the heavy stuff himself. My father is like that, too. A worker. Good with his hands."

My cell phone pulsed in my pocket. The call was early. I burst into the living room, interrupted their conversation. "You guys hear that? My phone is vibrating." I fished it from my pocket. "That's odd," I said, inspecting it. "I wonder who this is. A call at this time of the night? Wasn't expecting that." I swiped the screen and plugged my left ear with my finger, nodded a few times, said, "All right, sir, I understand, yes, okay, I'll be there," and ended the call with a sigh. "Damn, I was afraid this would happen. I apologize, you two, but I have to go."

"What?" Paige said. "What's going on?"

"They want me to come in."

"Who does?"

"Work. They're short staffed." I placed my hand on Mike's shoulder. "No, Mike, don't get up. Eat dinner with Paige."

"Declan," Paige said. "What are you doing?"

"They want me to come in." I rolled my eyes. "Perez says they're pulling an all-nighter in the office. Wish I could say no but let's face it, I'm a lowly functionary who can't afford to cross the wrong people."

Mike rose to his feet, preparing to head out. "Well," he said. "Some other time."

I laid a firm hand on his shoulder and shoved him back down. "Stay," I said. "All that delicious food. Shame to let it go to waste."

"For real?" Paige looked up at me. "You're leaving?"

"Bummer," Mike said.

"I agree with Mike's astute assessment," I said. "But don't let this little setback ruin the party. You two can still hang out. Oh man, I almost forgot." I darted into the kitchen and returned with a bottle of champagne. "Look what I found. Who wants bubbly? Here, Paige, pass these flutes around."

"Where did you get that?" she said.

"This bubbly?" I said, tilting the bottle to read the label. "It was just in the kitchen there, in one of the cabinets."

"No, it wasn't. I've never seen that bottle before. And stop saying 'bubbly.'"

I popped the cork, releasing a cascade of foam. "Hold out your glass, Mike," I said. "Attaboy. Right to the top." I filled Paige's glass as well. "There's two dozen oysters on ice in the kitchen and a free-range chicken roasting in the oven. Nothing to worry about."

Paige rose from the couch and smiled at our guest. "Excuse us for a minute, Mike." She followed me into the bedroom. "Dude. You're acting like a psycho. What's up?"

"Work. Always work." I grabbed my wallet and keys. "I'll be home by eleven-thirty." I kissed her forehead. "Midnight at the latest."

Before I left, I caught a glimpse of my fiancée's face. I paused. At that moment I wanted to drop to my knees, to confess, to put a stop to Phase One, but the plan was in motion. Paige, I reminded myself, would benefit in the end. That was all I'd ever wanted.

At a sports bar on Fifth Avenue, I took the stool next to Adam Kennedy, my big brother in Kappa Sig. I'd been out of college for almost a year but Adam continued to act as a sort of unofficial adviser and surrogate father. He was twenty-six years old, three years my senior, and the only person I confided in without reservation.

"Give me the rundown," he said. "Where we at?"

"Well, I think I found the guy. His name is Mike Balducci. They should be cutting into the chicken right about now."

"Balducci? Italian?" Adam Kennedy frowned. "Give me some stats."

I shrugged and waved to the bartender, who didn't see me or else ignored me. "Good-looking guy from my gym. Mid to late twenties. Medium height. Can bench press a ton. Wears a suit well. Doesn't talk much, though."

"Talking's not that important," Adam said. "Women don't care much about talking. Okay, we're in business. Phase Two begins this Friday. I hope Ballsacky is ready for this."

"Balducci," I said.

I frowned at my reflection behind the bottles, my face bisected by a groove where two mirrors had been joined. In Hollywood movies doom always awaited the two-faced man.

"Look, Adam," I said, "I'm having second thoughts about this."

"Perfectly natural," he said, not looking at me. "You'll get over that. Just stay the course."

"I'm serious. This doesn't feel right. I started with good intentions but Paige is a nice person, you know? An amazing person. Did you know that she—"

"That's cool." Adam motioned to the bartender with the slightest tilt of his head. Two more pints of beer arrived almost immediately. Adam took a long, thoughtful sip and wiped his lips with the back of his tie. "You'll be free of this entanglement in no time. I'm putting the Adam Kennedy guarantee on this. Have you been subtle like I told you?"

"You should have seen how I took your call tonight. Cool as ice. They don't suspect a thing. Even though you called early."

"Good. Perfect. I called right on time, by the way. And just before the game ends on Friday night"—he waved vaguely at the TV suspended above the bar—"we'll dial it up a notch for Phase Two."

I studied his face, the solid swoop of his jaw, the confident eyebrows. "What does that even mean?" I asked him. "Why won't you tell me everything at once?"

"Need-to-know basis, brother. Patent pending."

Adam Kennedy had always been secretive. Even in college, when the fraternity was giving out bids, all the other pledges knew before I did. Adam didn't tell me until the following morning, letting me sweat it out for an additional twelve hours. But say what you will, Adam Kennedy always got results. As a junior, he became fraternity president and increased our chapter's overall enrollment by forty percent. He was the first of our brothers in his graduating class to be offered a good job in Manhattan. At commencement he drove up in a brand new Range Rover while most of us were still riding single-gear bikes.

"What time did you tell her you'd be home?" Adam asked me.

"Midnight. I promised."

He laughed and glanced at his heavy gold wristwatch. "Roll in at four."

I drove around town for several hours. I stopped at a burger joint, threw darts at a biker bar, bowled three games at Melody Lanes, and stumbled into our apartment well after two o'clock in the morning. Paige was propped up in bed, reading *Modern Bride* magazine.

"How was your dinner with Mike?" I said.

"Where have you been?" She looked at me over her reading glasses. "I was worried about you."

I threw my keys and wallet on the dresser. "Did you enjoy dinner? How was Mike?"

"Whatever," she said. "He invited us to a Knicks game Friday. But I don't care about basketball."

"You would if you knew the rules. I bet Mike knows all the rules."

Paige put down her magazine. "You really like this guy, huh?"

"Michael Jordan? Michael 'row the boat ashore' Balducci? What's not to like?"

"I'm just saying. It's a little creepy. It's almost as if you're—"

"Okay, I admit it. I do feel kind of inadequate around him. And not just because Mike's hung like a horse, according to this guy named Karl at the gym. But Mike's brilliant, too. I think his IQ is something like 182."

"Those tests are totally inaccurate," she said and flicked a page of her magazine.

I dumped loose change on the dresser and reminded myself to be subtle. "Dozens of attractive women are chasing after Big

Mike Balducci. But Mike says he's waiting for the right gal. He's kind of old-fashioned that way. He believes in love, romance, a beautiful wedding by a lake, a fleet of limousines. He's a catch. He won't be single for long. Mike."

"Well, I guess we could go to the game. If you want to go." Paige grinned at me. She shut her magazine and laid it on the bedside table. "Unless you have something better planned."

"Me?" I laughed. "No, I can never think of anything fun to do."

I pulled off my shirt and sat down heavily on the bed. Bending over to untie my shoes, I knew that I was making big ugly gut rolls for her to look at.

On Friday afternoon around 3:30, I called Paige at work and told her I wouldn't make it to the basketball game.

"Why?"

"Work. That's all I ever seem to do, to the exclusion of all my loved ones."

"Well, whatever," she said. "Call what's-his-balls and tell him we can't go. I can't say that I really care. Basketball's not my cup of—"

"Oh, but those tickets are so expensive," I said. "And I bet they're great seats, knowing Mike. Probably one of the starting players hooked him up. No, no, you'd better go with him."

"What? I don't want to go to a Knicks game on a Friday night with Mike!"

"You think I like it? I hate it. I'll be so jealous. Both of your hands in the same bag of popcorn. But what can we do? Think about poor Mike."

"Why doesn't 'poor Mike' take one of his numerous lady friends with him?"

"Let's not hurt his feelings," I said. "Mike's sensitive. He's strong but sensitive. That's what you might not understand about him. Mike's an enigma. Nobody knows the full story of Mike. The book of Mike is a mystery novel waiting for an intelligent female reader to deconstruct."

"Are you shitting me?" she said. "Look, I can't talk right now. I have work to do."

"What I'm saying is don't judge a book by its cover. You're looking at Mike and seeing a muscular, athletic, handsome man, and you're not alone. People in the gym stop and watch him dead lift. He's that strong. But Mike's sensitive too, and this might hurt his feelings. If we both turn our backs on him now, he might not go to the game at all. He might stay at home, thinking we don't like him anymore."

"Is this some kind of prank?" she said. "This is getting so weird, Declan."

"I'm the one that's weird." I nodded in agreement. "I'm flighty and moody and kind of a kook. Unstable as all get out. But Mike? He's solid and dependable."

She hung up.

Five hours later, at the bar, I gave Adam the rundown. "Phase Two is in effect. Very smooth transition. She's at Madison Square Garden with Mike."

"Nice work, bro."

"So what's the next part of your exit strategy?"

Adam motioned to the bartender, held up two fingers. "Time to talk Phase Three." He glanced left and right, making sure that nobody was eavesdropping. "I call it Bound and Gagged."

Two beers arrived. The bartender plucked a few bills off Adam's stack and moved away again.

"We'll watch the Knick game here," Adam said. "Toward the end of the fourth quarter we'll go back to your apartment and smash the shit out of everything. Then I'll tie you up and slap you around a bit."

"Now, wait a second," I said.

"Trust me, bro," Adam said, watching the game over my head. "I don't like it any more than you do, but it's essential."

"Yeah, but—"

"I'm doing this for you, goddammit. My ex-girlfriends have all moved on without blaming me at all. They think *they* broke up with me. They think they hurt *my* feelings."

"But why does this have to be so . . . you know . . . macho?"

Adam flicked a peanut off the bar. "You should chat with a Vietnam vet who was airlifted out of Saigon and tell him you think my exit strategy is a little too *macho*." He pulled out his cell phone. "You know what? I'll get my uncle Frank on the horn. The man's missing a leg. Tell Frank what you think."

"Jesus, don't call any disabled veterans." I grabbed the phone out of his hands and laid it on the bar. "I'm listening."

He snatched up his phone and polished it with a drink napkin. "Nobody touches Adam's phone," he said. "Nobody."

"So you tie me up," I said, trying to calm him down. "Fine. Great. And then what?"

"You sack up like a goddamn soldier and wait for your backup. When they see you like that, completely emasculated, you've already got one foot out the door. Super Mike storms onto the scene, unties you, consoles Paige, and three months from now, the Italian Stallion rides to victory in your former bed."

"In my bed? Mike Balducci?"

"Shit yeah. You've moved out by then. You think they'll go to hotel rooms out of respect for you?"

I didn't like the sound of that. I didn't like the sound of any of it! Paige was not some pawn to be used in such a brutal game. Emotional intimacy was certainly difficult and maybe even impossible for me, but I didn't want her to suffer for it. The truth was, I just wanted Paige to be happy and contented and adored by a partner who didn't have my glaring defects of character, my immaturity, and my meager earning potential.

Adam's pint of beer was empty. He glared at mine, still half full.

"And then what happens?" I said. "Mike moves in. Paige marries him instead. Remind me what I'm getting out this again."

"Oh, just a little thing called freedom," Adam said. "How does that sound, hero?"

The gym sock was clean. I insisted on that, even though Adam wanted to use the dirtiest one—"for verisimilitude," he argued.

I sat on a stiff wooden chair in my living room. Adam tied both of my hands behind my back with a bungee cord. Then he shoved the gym sock in my mouth and wrapped duct tape three or four times around my head.

I gagged.

The tape was too tight, and I grunted to indicate this, but Adam ignored my pleas. "Close your eyes and brace yourself," he said. The punch came before I expected it, his rough knuckles pounding my right cheekbone and eye socket. Pain shot through my body. My right eyelid burned hot, as if he'd taken a scalpel to it.

Shaking it off, I watched in horror as Adam ransacked our kitchen. He poured orange juice on the floor, lit all the dishtowels on fire, and kicked over a six-tiered bookcase, scattering our books. He swept my laptop off the kitchen counter onto the floor. He stomped our coffee table into splinters.

"This is starting to look real," he said, his eyes dark and wild. "Yo, Dec, which closet is Paige's?" He headed toward the back of the apartment. "And where does she keep her panties?"

I rocked from side to side, growling into the sock, but my objections went unheeded.

A few minutes later, Adam returned to the kitchen with a smile on his face. He removed deli-wrapped envelopes of ham and cheese from the refrigerator and built himself a towering sandwich, three layers high, with sliced tomatoes and ruffles of romaine lettuce. He slathered on mayo and mustard. He pillaged a twelve-pack of beer, tucking it under his arm. Then he swung open the door, calling out, "Sit tight, hero. This is going to work like a charm. Trust me."

I tried to free my hands but the knots were too tight. For two hours I had no choice but to stare at the wreckage of my life. I wondered if there were any better ways to handle it. Should I have risked a thorny conversation with my fiancée?

I suppose I could have said, "Paige, I love you, but I might not be ready to get married yet. I'm scared, that's all. We're just so young, you know? I think we should maybe slow down. What do you think?" But I loved her too much to hurt her like that.

My eyelid had swollen shut. My wrists burned. Minutes ticked off the clock while I waited for them to return.

Finally, the door opened. I couldn't believe it. Paige was alone.

"Oh, my God," she said, rushing to me. She untied my hands and removed the whisker-uprooting tape and pulled the sock out of my mouth. "Oh, oh, oh," she said, hugging me. "Are you okay, babe? What happened?"

"Where's Mike?" I said, gasping for air. "Is he parking his cool BMW?"

"What?"

"Balducci!" I said, my voice ragged. "Where is he?"

"Dropped me off. Told him I had a headache. Oh, baby, now I know why you didn't show up. We were both so worried about you. I'm sorry that I got angry with you. I didn't know!"

I looked at her through my one good eye. "How was your night? Did Mike take you out for a cocktail or dancing after dinner?"

She shook her head.

That cheap son of a bitch, I thought. "He just dropped you off?" I rubbed my abraded cheek. "Didn't he even try to kiss you?"

"Kiss me? Of course not. He was a perfect gentleman."

I nodded, smiled. "Didn't I tell you he was a gentleman? Mike's old-fashioned. And women respond to that. He was dating this model for a while before she moved back to Barcelona. Keep it under your hat. Mike's pretty modest about that kind of stuff."

Paige bent down and cupped my face in her hands. "Your poor face! Should I take you to the hospital?"

"No, I'm coolio."

"Call the cops right now. How many were there?"

"Just one," I said. "One little guy."

"Can you make a positive identification?"

"Oh yeah. I'd know that miniature bastard anywhere. He was probably five-five with a receding chin, a milky left eye, and a deformed right arm. It was like a flipper. You know, like, hanging off his shoulder?"

"Really?" she said, baffled. "Jeez. What did he want? Why did he break in?"

"I don't know. I was hiding under the bed and he pulled me out by the ankles."

Paige chewed her lower lip and laid her hand on my chest. "Call the cops."

"Nope," I said, smiling at her. "I have a better idea. I'll call our mutual friend, Mister Deadlift himself."

Paige and I cleaned up the place as best we could, but the intruder had caused a lot of damage. A framed photo montage of her family—brothers, sister, parents—had been shattered beneath Adam Kennedy's boot heel. She held the pieces in her hands and cried.

I bent over her, pressed the back of my hand to her hot cheek. I felt compelled to admit my duplicity, and I started to say something—"Paige, listen,"—but I was interrupted by a knock on the door, which she had left ajar.

"Mike!" I said, spotting Paige's future husband in the doorway. "Come on in, my man. We've been waiting for you."

"Dude," Mike said, looking around at the scene. I nodded, waited for more. "Duuuude," Mike added.

"Look at this mess!" Paige said. "Can you believe it?" On her hands and knees she looked up at us, her two men, with an expression of murderous rage on her face. For a moment she had stopped being sympathetic to my plight—my recent brush with an intruder—and had moved on to rage at the midget aggressor. "Little bastard smashed my pictures."

"Bummer. They steal anything?" Mike asked. The sleuth was on duty.

"Perceptive question, Mike," I said. "No. Strangely enough. They—he—didn't steal anything. Except, well, a ham and cheese sandwich and some domestic beer."

Paige looked up from the floor, blinking her teary eyes. "What? Are you fucking kidding me?"

"We shouldn't fixate on all the details," I said.

Paige couldn't let it go. "He made a sandwich? After he tied you to a chair and smashed my pictures?"

"They have no respect for personal property," Mike said. "They think they deserve welfare checks and government handouts, but maybe they should try working for a living."

Paige's mouth fell open. She looked at Mike, then at me, trying to process everything at once.

"Whoa, Mike," I said. "Let's not jump to any unfounded conclusions here."

"I blame Barack *Hussein* Obama for all the entitlements," Mike said.

"Heh-heh," I said. "I think what Mike's *trying* to say—"

"Prison isn't enough for some of them," Mike said, nodding. "They seem to love it there. So maybe we need to impose stricter measures."

Jesus, was Mike a straight-up racist asshole? How had I missed that during my stringent locker-room vetting process?

"Rehabilitation?" Mike went on. "More like three hots and a cot. Club Med."

I had to stop him. Paige's family wouldn't stand for that crap. Not at all. And neither would I.

I had no choice but to view this as a teachable moment.

"First of all, Mike, let's stop saying 'they,'" I suggested, angling my face toward him, so I could see him with my unswollen eye. "That's only confusing matters. It was just one dude.

Just a tiny Caucasian guy in flip-flops and a poncho. Second of all—"

"He was wearing flip-flops and a fucking poncho?" Paige stared at me. "For real?"

"The *point* is," I said, my voice cracking with frustration, "the point is we have *each other*. Right, Mike? Paige? We're safe. Nobody is trying to hurt us anymore because Mike Balducci is here."

"You gotta call the cops," Mike said.

"That's what I told him," Paige said, nodding at Mike. "I told him that half an hour ago."

I put my hands on my hips and smiled at the two of them. "It's uncanny how you two always think alike. Look at me, you two, I'm still shaking." I held out my hand and wriggled my fingers. "I don't trust my own decision-making right now. You too should put your heads together and confer. If you need privacy, you can go in the bedroom and shut the door. Cuddle up and discuss my screwed-up and frankly embarrassing situation."

"I'm calling the cops," Paige said.

"Good idea," Mike said. "That's what I would do."

I laughed and shook my finger at them. "You guys," I said.

The police officers arrived an hour later, two stocky guys in their thirties who couldn't have looked more bored. They strutted in wearing their full gear—guns, pepper spray, cuffs, etc. "So who called about the break-in?"

I raised my shaky hand. "I did, officer." Slumped in the armchair, I had an afghan draped over my lap. "Little old me."

Beside me on the end table was a mug of Earl Grey tea from Paige. She was such a thoughtful person, empathetic, and for a moment I envied Mike.

I gave the cops a precise description of the freckled red-headed perp. I said the flipper rested on the poncho's fabric like "a mammoth slug on a picnic blanket," and I was mildly disappointed when they didn't write that simile down in their notepads.

The cops said they'd see what they could do. With the afghan wrapped around my shoulders I escorted them out.

"Good luck, officers," Mike called out. "Sounds like this particular criminal will be easy to find. The rest of 'em are probably harder to spot in the dark."

One of the cops, a biracial man, turned and said, "Excuse me? What did you just say?"

I stepped neatly between them. "We've all been through a lot tonight, officer. Forgive my friend. He's undeniably handsome and popular with the ladies and makes enough money to satisfy any woman, but sometimes he speaks out of turn."

The cop looked at me and narrowed his eyes. "Yeah," he said. "We'll let you know if we find anything."

After they left, I headed for the bedroom, barely lifting my feet. "Gonna lie down," I said. "Really bushed. Doesn't take much to rattle a guy like me."

"Anything I can do?" Mike asked. The champ. I knew he'd come through sooner or later.

I turned to Paige. "Do you feel safe staying here tonight, honey? Would you rather go somewhere else?" Then I looked pointedly at Mike. "A hotel would probably be too expensive."

Mike coughed into his fist. "I'd better get going," he said.

I put my hand out to stop him. "Want to crash on the couch, buddy? I don't presume to speak for Paige, but I think we'd both feel better if a man was here."

"Nah," Mike said. "I'll just head back to my condo."

Paige smiled at him. "Good night, Mike." She took hold of his elbow and walked him to the door. "Thanks for stopping by. We both appreciate it."

"Yeah, just—you know." He shrugged. "All right. Cool."

"And thanks for dinner," she added. "It was fun—considering."

They looked at each other. This was Mike's big opportunity. The door to her heart was wide open. Would the swain deliver?

Mike cleared his throat. I tiptoed closer, hunched under the afghan. Paige and I both endured a tantalizing moment of suspense.

"Well, okay," Mike said at last, twirling his car keys on his finger. "Later."

Disappointing. No other way to put it. I made a mental note to buy Mike a pocket thesaurus.

In retrospect, the truth was obvious. Paige deserved better than this. Frankly, I deserved better. That night I decided to tell Adam Kennedy that Mike Balducci was out of the running in the marriage sweepstakes.

What I hadn't planned on, however, was losing my job. "Sorry, hombre," my manager Brett said, bouncing a superball against his office wall. "Nothing personal. We're all on thin ice here, including yours truly." He caught the ball and tossed it again. "I'll probably be right behind you on the unemployment line."

While my coworkers averted their eyes, I cleaned out my desk and dumped everything in the trash. All of that useless, disposable junk—why had I cared about any of it? I walked out of the building in a daze, empty-handed and unemployed.

For a week I refused to believe that my termination had anything to do with my abilities or my character. Cutbacks were unavoidable, I told myself. The economy was in bad shape. I made thirty phone calls and tried to cash in favors but my friends couldn't hook me up, and all those bullshit websites like LinkedIn, Twitter, Facebook, and Craigslist were full of dead ends. How did people find jobs these days?

Demoralized, I spent mornings on the couch with the remote control in my hand, watching game shows and soap operas. I scooped butter pecan ice cream straight from the carton. Unshowered, unshaved, I moped around our apartment in my black bathrobe. I gained twelve pounds and couldn't muster the energy for sit-ups or push-ups, let alone a trip to the gym. My life slowed to a grinding halt, and I realized how important Paige was to me. I couldn't wait for her to get home at night.

Mike Balducci called a few times, saying he hadn't seen me at the gym, but I told him to leave us alone. "You got us into this mess in the first place," I told him. "I'll take it from here, thank you very much."

During this time of doubt and turmoil, I leaned on Paige, my pillar, my greatest support. I had made some mistakes in the past, sure, but all married couples weathered storms, and I looked forward to sharing our own. "Oh, we had some rough times at the beginning," they always said, smiling at one another and reaching for the other's hand. Precisely! And so had we!

It took me a while, over a month, to acclimate to unemployment. With what little remained of my savings I bought Paige flowers and chocolates. I told her I couldn't wait to marry her. I offered her back rubs at night. I asked if I could rub her feet, too.

"I'm tired," she said. "Let's just go to sleep, Declan. Okay?"

While she was at work, I vacuumed the apartment. I did loads of laundry. I looked up recipes online and cooked sumptuous feasts with ingredients from the co-op. I investigated honeymoon locales and prepared pros and cons lists for each. Reception themes? Countless options.

When Paige returned from work at night, I barraged her with chitchat after another day alone in the apartment. "You should have seen this three-legged dog at the post office—so cute!" I followed her from room to room. "How do you feel about Belize for our honeymoon?" I joined her in the kitchen. "I'm really beginning to understand jazz. It's really coming alive to me on a personal level, you know?" I cornered her in the bedroom. "Can you look at this thing on the back of my neck? What is it?"

Paige came home later and later at night, which was understandable because of the big project she told me she was working on. Sometimes she went out with her girlfriends directly from work. A few times, more than once, she called me at midnight and warned me not to wait up.

"But I made paella," I said the last time it happened.

I waited up anyway. And I confronted her when she returned at dawn, stumbling in with her hair snarled and her skirt askew. "Who were you with?" I said. "What were you doing? Why didn't you call?"

"I told you I went dancing. *Danshing*," she slurred.

When Paige suggested we postpone the wedding, I choked back tears and asked why. "I'm only twenty-four," she said.

"That's not that young."

"Thanks, Declan." She walked into the bathroom. "You say the sweetest things sometimes."

Most nights she refused to have sex with me, claiming she was tired, or her breasts hurt, or she'd just eaten a huge burger, or she had a rib injury, or there was a supermoon.

"Suit yourself!" I stormed out of the bedroom and slept on the couch.

Then, one night, Paige dropped the bomb. She told me she'd bumped into our old friend Mike Balducci at a nightclub and they'd danced together.

"That loser?" I said. "Did he bore you to death?"

"What are you saying? You love Mike. You're the one who made me see his good qualities. He's conservative, but kind. In a way he reminds me of my grandfather."

"Mike is dumber than this pillow," I said, slapping my hand on it for emphasis.

"You said Mike had a high IQ."

"Did I? I was thinking of somebody else. Mike was held back in eighth grade. And he abuses animals. And he tips five percent in restaurants. Mike Balducci is bad news."

She looked beautiful with her glossy black hair washed and pinned up on her head. I remembered the first day I saw her in psych class. She wore a camouflage tank top with spaghetti straps. Her cheap aviator sunglasses, hooked on the neckline, dead center, pulled down the worn cotton fabric to reveal crescents of white skin just below her tan line. When she crossed her legs and hitched her sarong to mid-calf, I noticed her bare ankle, the sandal dangling from her bobbing toe, and the mosquito bite she'd picked until it developed a scab. I made a mental note to buy calamine lotion and cotton balls.

Who needed an exit strategy? Not me. This was shaping up to be, by far, the worst mistake of my life. I felt powerless to stop what I'd set in motion.

"Belize is beautiful at this time of the year!" I said. "It's beautiful and we're going to see it as man and wife."

Paige told me I needed to see a therapist.

Instead, I met with Adam Kennedy at the sports bar and told him what was happening.

"Solid gold," Adam said, patting me on the back. "Won't be long now."

"But I love Paige." I listed her good qualities and related anecdotes that revealed her strength of character, describing the type of woman any man would like to spend his life with. How foolish I'd been!

Paige and I were both Libras born four days apart in September, which, according to her, meant that we were often incapable of deciding what to eat for dinner or which movies to watch. When we moved in together and consolidated our books, we found that they were too numerous to keep in a cramped, three-room apartment. All the shelves were packed. We had a lot of duplicates. Corners were overrun with teetering stacks of paperbacks. But being Libras, we couldn't decide which ones to chuck and which ones to keep.

I felt relief to have been awarded an astrological explanation for my lifelong inability to get shit done. And Paige had given that to me. She explained that Libras were extremists, prone to black-and-white thinking. The misconception most people had was that Libras were balanced people—hence, the scales. People thought that if there were twelve of one thing—cookies, say—Libras would split them up into equal groups of six and six. But what it really meant, according to Paige, was that Libras would hoard all twelve or take none at all. They *needed* balance; they didn't *have* balance. While she talked about this connection we shared, I admired the zigzag part in her shiny black hair, the glyph she erased and reconfigured from time to time by raking her hand through it. It was October. She was still tanned from summer, but the brown freckled skin on her shoulders had started to peel. I wanted to help her exfoliate.

I said all this to Adam.

"Agreed," he said. "She's a great catch for Mike Ballsacky."

"She's a great catch for me!" I said.

"Negative," he said. "You could do better."

Paige began sleeping at her mom's house in Floral Park. She said she wanted to spend more time with her family. I couldn't get her on her cell phone. When I called the house, her mom said Paige was taking a nap or playing with her nieces and didn't want to be disturbed.

I drove past the house every night, not in a stalkerish way but as a future husband who was focused on her well-being. I parked across the street and watched through the picture window. Her father read the newspaper in the living room every night. Her mother read a book. Her sister smiled a lot. What a great family! And, God, wasn't Paige beautiful? When she got down on the floor and played board games with her nieces, I admired her skill with children. I wanted so badly to be inside the house with them, drinking Salada tea and eating Hydrox cookies. I would have done anything to get her back. Anything.

One night in April I was parked across the street, eating my dinner, when Adam Kennedy pulled up in a customized van. Big pieces of cardboard were taped over the side windows. I wondered how Adam knew I was there. And where was his Range Rover? I was about to call out to him, to warn him he was blowing my cover, when he jumped out of the van and hurried up the walk with a bouquet of flowers in his fist.

I tumbled out of my car, spilling my carryout meatloaf and mashed potatoes in the process, and darted across the front lawn. I confronted my co-conspirator before he rang the bell. "What are you doing?" I said. "You're gonna ruin everything."

The look of surprise on Adam's face was quickly replaced by placidity. "Oh, hey. Didn't see you there. What's up?" He looked down at the red carnations in his hand. "This is all part of our strategy. Phase Five."

"There is no more strategy. I decided I'm going to marry Paige after all."

Adam rang the bell again. "Too late for that."

"Get out of here." I shoved him. "Go."

"You're in too deep, soldier," Adam said. "You can't evacuate from a Five-Phase exit strategy now. It would be a disaster. Who knows how many civilians will be affected?"

"Watch me." I rang the doorbell. "Watch the sparks fly."

"This is a quagmire," Adam said and rang the bell.

We heard Mike's car only after it was parked. He had pulled up in his cherry-red BMW. I took in his dark suit, the open-necked shirt, and the handkerchief neatly folded in his breast pocket. He, too, was carrying flowers.

"Froggy comes a-courtin', eh?" Adam said with a nervous giggle.

"Not now, Mike." I held out my hand, palm vertical, fingers pointing at the sky. "Stop right there."

"What are you doing here?" Mike said with genuine surprise. "And who's this?"

The front door of the house opened. Paige appeared behind the glass of the storm door, dressed in a nice blouse and a skirt I didn't recognize.

"A full-blown quagmire," Adam said.

Mike Balducci tried to step past us but I grabbed him and held him back. Adam shoved us both. I tightened my bear hug on Mike, who was still clutching his bouquet of cherry blossoms.

"Go home," I grunted in his ear. "You're out of your depths."

"Get off me," Mike said.

"Kill him," Adam said to one or both of us.

Paige slapped her palm against the glass. "Stop, you idiots."

Her family members joined her in the vestibule, the father in reading glasses, the mother holding a cup of dice.

Civilians gathered on the sidewalk. They didn't know what to do. A child on a leash dropped his tennis ball and cried. His mother pressed him to her thighs and covered his face with her hands, but he had already seen too much.

"Look at yourselves," Paige said to us. "What is wrong with you guys?"

The first punch came from Adam, a haymaker that connected with the force of a club. Pink petals spilled over the flagstone.

I heard shouting and screams from every direction. Torn green tissue paper fluttered across the lawn. For a moment, I didn't know who to help or where to pledge my allegiance.

While Adam subdued Mike with a vicious chokehold, Paige waved me over to the door for a private lover's chat.

Finally, an opportunity to make things right!

I apologized to her for Mike and Adam's behavior. "They should be ashamed of themselves," I said loud enough for her father to hear. "Your family deserves better."

"No sweat," she said. "Stuff happens."

I couldn't have said it better myself. "You're amazing," I told her.

"Hey, I know you love live music. You know who else does? My co-worker Savannah."

"Paige, listen to me. This whole thing, this mess—everything got way out of hand."

"Savannah's new in town and needs someone to show her around. Can I give her your number? I think you'll really like her."

APPETITES

Kafka fingers his begonias. He bends over them and frowns. I am seated on a lawn chair nearby, slurping a Long Island Iced Tea through a bent yellow straw. "Franz, what are we doing here, I ask you?" I ask him. He does not reply, merely spritzes the waxy leaves with the pump sprayer in his leather garden glove. "Guys like us," I say, "we should be out boozing and brawling, picking up chicks." Kafka drops to his hands and knees to inspect the soil. "With your ears and chin," I continue, "my biceps and hairline, we would be unstoppable, my man." Kafka ignores me.

Kafka on his motorcycle, speeding recklessly through the city. I am navigating from the sidecar. A crimson scarf flaps jauntily in the wind behind me. "Turn left here," I say. Both wearing goggles, we are headed to the Stumble Inn for chicken wings and darts. Franz is meeting a chick named Sherry. She claims to have a friend for me. "Is mine cute, Franz?" I yell over the rushing wind. Gloved fists gripping the handlebars, Kafka ignores me, and flicks his wrist. I feel the acceleration in the pit of my stomach. Buildings blur beside us. Lips moving without voices. Pedestrians, road crews, stray dogs.

We meet the chicks at the bar. They're already drunk and don't understand our jokes and witty banter. Sherry, the shorter one, has an unfortunate tattoo on her left forearm: MEATLOAF WORLD TOUR '82. She drinks Jack. Janelle's lime green tank top appears to be crusted with vomit. She says "fuck" a lot and drinks bottled beer.

Kafka and I have a checkered history with women, probably because we want them to take all of our pain away and carry it for us, while we remain focused on our special projects behind closed doors, chasing immortality. We heap our psychic pain on women's backs like sacks of grain because we are too weak to carry the load ourselves. This does not increase our popularity or make us intriguing candidates for marriage.

At 2:30 in the morning, Kafka pilots his motorcycle away from the Stumble Inn. He said the wrong things again and scared the chicks away. Hunched over the handlebars, goggles strapped on, Kafka sublimates with speed. My scarf is whipping above my head. Like a man cut free from a noose.

In the bathtub, Kafka has a death grip on my rubber toad. "Franz, take it easy on Mister Toad, would ya?" He tosses it onto the floor. It squeaks and comes to a halt near the brown wicker clothes hamper. We sit in silence. "Franz, hand me the soap," I say. He does not move a muscle. "The soap, Franz," I say. "Hand. Me. The. Soap." Kafka turns his head away. His bony chest and rib cage heave with each breath he takes. Angry silence. We do not look at each other for a minute or two. "It was my toad," I say finally. "If it was yours, fine. You have to treat other people's things nicer." Kafka ignores me.

In his presence I feel windblown, flighty. On the beach I ask him questions that I know he can't answer, but I cannot refrain from speaking incessantly. "Why do dogs chase their tails? What do you like about the theory of relativity? Are you thinking about me as much as I'm thinking about you?"

I'm fumbling in my pockets for change. I've just purchased two Nutty Buddys, one for me, one for Franz.

Now I have both ice creams in one hand and I reach out the other hand, the hand with the money, reaching out and angling my torso forward at the same time, careful not to jar my paperback loose from my armpit. The pages, I notice with some aggravation, are still damp with bathwater. "Renovations," says the ice cream man, accepting the money from me. He nods at something over my shoulder. "Right," I say, confused. I don't know what he's talking about. "Long time coming," he says. "Taxpayer dollars." "Well." I shrug back. "What're you gonna do?" "Grin and bear it." He hands me a tiny napkin. "Thanks," I say. Walking away, I hoist my ice creams in a toast. "Nice talking to you." "You too, buddy."

Nobody knows me like Franz does. He understands pain, loneliness. The two of us sit quietly on this wooden bench. We are licking, chewing, not speaking, watching the sun set orange over the purple pier. There is no cause to be frightened. We are safe here. No one is allowed to hurt us here. Enjoy the ice cream, enjoy the light. It's been another good day. Women are not the key to our happiness. "We need to learn to love ourselves," I say. Solitude enhances self-awareness. Kafka nods and licks off a creamy white 'stache of vanilla ice cream. I watch his eyes. I know what he's thinking and I turn my head. "Where?" I ask him. And then I see her too, long legs swishing together, approaching where we sit.

THE WIND IN THE STREET

A muggy night in August. I'm hanging out in Molly's cramped apartment on Fifth Avenue in Brooklyn. A hot breeze blows through the open windows, rippling the once-white curtains. It has only just stopped raining.

"We need more beer," Molly says, staring into the blue glow of her laptop. She's working on a status update. Her nose ring sparkles in the dim glare of the naked bulb overhead. She taps my knee and smiles, making eye contact for the first time in half an hour. "Will you go buy some?"

I still have a lot of work to do tonight. I stopped by Molly's only to say a quick what's up before digging in to my own work.

"Get a twelve-pack," she says. "There's money in my purse." She waves her hand to indicate a non-cyber world where a purse might exist.

"I have a lot to do tonight."

"Don't say that." Finally she looks up at me, pouts. I've known her since elementary school. When she was ten, her black hair was bobbed and clipped back with a yellow barrette. She wore Lee jeans and western blouses. We all wanted to poke her with our no. 2 pencils. "There's a bodega on the next corner."

"That's not the point."

"They've gotta be kidding," she says to the screen. "A unitard? That's ridiculous."

Molly wears too-small T-shirts that expose her midriff and expensive jeans slung low on her hips, her peach or purple underwear always visible in the back. She looks away from the screen long enough to flash me a smile. "It's just a block away," she says.

I stare at the opposite wall. A rickety metal fan rattles on high speed in the open window, blowing in pizza and garbage smells from outside. Empty beer bottles and sticky glasses crowd the coffee table, the tops of speakers, the kitchenette counters. A change of scenery might not be so bad. A promenade might inspire me in some unpredictable way. I'll just have to work a little later tonight, that's all.

I stand up and head to the door. "Fine."

Molly smiles approvingly at her laptop. "You're awesome."

Outside her building, a bearded man in sunglasses squats in the doorway of a vintage clothes shop. He's dressed in a heavy overcoat with a dirty gray fur collar, wool trousers, and yellow flip-flops. "Raaaaa," he says to me. "My name is Lucifer, the Prince of Darkness, and I am very very scary. Fear my wrath. For I am Lucifer. Raaaa, raaaaa."

A car alarm clamors on the next block.

"Don't you walk away from Lucifer," he shouts at my back. "Give Lucifer a quarter."

I don't have any change. "I'll give you something on the way back," I call out over my shoulder.

"You're lying!"

"No. I promise. I'm just heading to the bodega to buy beer."

"In the book of Revelation . . ." he begins, but I have no time to stop and chat about religious doctrine. I bolt across the street as the traffic signal turns yellow.

"Do that again, Beansy, and I'll kick your fucking ass," a man shouts outside a bar.

"Yeah?" another man (presumably Beansy) responds, taunting him. "Bring it."

There is a palpable feeling of malice on the street. Men are everywhere, in doorways and in parked cars, doing nothing and thrilled about it. Cruel, furtive eyes. Suspicious glances.

"Hey hey, dude. Wanna buy some weed?" A teenager with bleached hair and black sideburns waves to me from across the street. "I got the kind bud, fella."

I take a little detour. "Weed, huh? How old are you kids?"

"Seven hundred years old," the blond kid says.

"Yo, this is the wheelchair weed, son," his freckled buddy says. This one's the muscle, the redheaded enforcer, a scowling child in a Kangol cap and Timberland boots. "Two hits and you're paralyzed."

"Perhaps I'll stop in for a moment," I say. "But I'm heading to the bodega, gentlemen. My girlfriend Molly is waiting for me. Well, she's not my girlfriend technically, but we have a connection that—Anyway. And more importantly I have quite a bit of work to do tonight. It's looking like it's going to be an all-nighter."

The ginger peckerwood holds the front door open for me. "You're going for a ride, Knievel."

His bravado is oddly touching.

The blond kid introduces himself as Smokes. He talks about himself in a manic, high-pitched voice: his folks are on vacation for a week in Cancun; he's a really good drummer; his band kicks major ass; they sold out the community center up in Golden's Bridge.

His freckled friend treats me to an array of savage looks, heavy-lidded and disapproving. His jeans are clownishly loose and puddled around his ankles. He has to hitch them up when he steps in any direction.

I follow him inside, my boot soles sticking to the kitchen's linoleum floor.

I take two or three hits of the weed and a full hour passes before I'm able to speak again. When my tongue no longer feels like a slumbering gerbil in my mouth, I try to push myself up from the couch. I am vaguely aware that Smokes has been on the phone for some time now, cajoling a nearby pajama party to switch locations. He's speaking in a complex patois that is beyond me. His bodyguard has disappeared. It's possible that I fell into a temporary coma. I can't get off the couch.

When six high school girls sway through the front door without knocking or ringing the bell, I feel suddenly like a creepy chaperone or a prehistoric hominid primate lounging on the couch. *Australopithecus Robustus*.

"Hey, Smokes!" they call out. "What's up, sexy?"

The apartment door bangs behind them. All but one of them are tall, scrawny, heavily made-up teenagers with durable hair and prominent breasts. They're attractive in their way, but the one who intrigues me most is short, squat, and sullen. No make-up or jewelry. She wears a baggy peasant blouse and ragged sandals. She straggles behind the others.

Despite the lingering numbness in my legs, I escape to the kitchen where I mix myself a drink. "I have work to do," I say aloud. "Why won't anyone let me get my work done?"

Smokes cranks the stereo in the living room. I hear the opening notes of *Blood Sugar Sex Magik* by the Red Hot Chili Peppers. "A golden oldie going out to my man," he announces in a voice loud enough for me to hear. Smokes waves me into the living room—"Yo, son, come meet these bitches"—but I remain where I am, chopping a lime on the cutting board. I've decided to build a margarita, something gay and festive to keep my spirits up in these challenging times, but when I discover that there is no tequila in the liquor cabinet, I'm crestfallen. Why do I even bother? Eventually I locate a full bottle of Tanqueray gin, and I recover my mirth. "Good to be alive," I say aloud.

The short hippie girl—Ashley—joins me shortly after I've made myself a cocktail.

Ashley has a round and ruddy face and a radiant smile as close to perfection as anyone could wish, but she suppresses it as one would a nasty secret. Too much will have to change in the world before Ashley will smile freely. She scowls instead and talks about migrant workers in Mexico as if they're her favorite old uncles.

"Look at them," she says with disdain, sweeping out her arm to implicate her peers in the living room, "they have no conception of true oppression and hardship. Three billion people in the world make less than five bucks a day. But here"—and she casts her dazzling critical gaze at me—"here they just waste and waste and waste."

I sip my Tanqueray-and-tonic. "True," I say, "but they're just kids, Ashley. Once you get older, into your mid-twenties, like me, partying becomes a lot less important. You realize that you have work to do."

She says, "I just want to get away from everything."

"I hear you, sister." I raise my G & T in toast. "You're preaching to the choir now."

She scrutinizes my face. "America sucks," she says, her gray eyes gleaming. Her lashes are long, lovely. "We're on a crash course for cataclysm. No hands on the wheel. It's all smoke and mirrors. Doesn't matter who is president." She glares at me as if I've had something to do with it.

"Mm-hm," I say.

In the living room, Smokes brings a joint up to his lips. He sucks on it with great force, his eyes closed. The ember glows, brilliant orange. A seed pops. Tiny black flakes of paper see-saw to the floor. His voice emerges from somewhere deep in his throat. "Smokes is in da house."

"I want to live in the woods," Ashley says to me. "Grow my own vegetables."

"Sounds nice." I swig my drink. "I could get into something like that myself. A fresh start. Get some frigging work done."

Ashley rakes her hand through her long auburn hair, and she leans against the countertop to get a better look at me. "Are you serious, man? Because I know a place we could go. Tonight. I've been thinking about it for months."

"Sounds totally feasible," I say, smiling tolerantly at her dreams. Once you get to my age, you realize that your life is basically already over. But you can still appreciate the naïve hopefulness of a teenager who hasn't yet been vanquished.

"Listen, Ashley," I say, "it was nice meeting you. Good luck with everything. My girlfriend Molly is waiting for me.

Well, technically, she's not my girlfriend. I mean, Molly doesn't really like to be tied down by labels or obligations, and I totally respect her independence, but I think it's fair to say we're good close friends, considering the amount of physical intimacy we've shared over the years."

"I knew you wouldn't have the guts."

"Yeah, it's just—well, somebody has to go out and buy the beer while Molly is checking her Facebook and Twitter and Instagram and her blogs and stuff."

"We won't need modern crap like that where we're heading, man. The only thing we'll need to worry about is hunting, survival." She drains her drink and leaves the cup on the counter. "You ready? Just follow me." She walks right past her friends in the living room, as if she has never seen them before.

I follow behind her, suspecting that we'll soon turn around on the sidewalk, amused by our little joke, and rejoin the party.

As her Toyota Corolla wheezes down the BQE, Ashley regales me with tales of her early years. Strapped into the shotgun seat, I sip my sploshing G & T and stare out the window. I had the foresight to freshen up my cocktail before heading out the door. After her folks died, she says, her grandparents raised her in Portland, Oregon. "I hated it there. They treated me like a pet." Finally, she met an older man, an anarchist poet named Geoff, and he showed her a whole new life. Soon she was living in an abandoned building with a faction of young radicals in Eugene.

"I never felt so alive," she says, turning to me. "We caused a lot of damage. I can't really go into the specifics."

"That's okay," I say. "Just watch the road."

"I learned how to make my frustrations felt on a grand scale."

"Wow, that's . . ."

Half an hour passes. In the passenger seat I nurse my drink. Despite my efforts, I can't make it last and lean my head against the window and doze off for a few hours. Dreaming. A childhood friend presses a bowie knife to my throat. "Don't cry," he says. Gravel crunches beneath the tires. Her Corolla shudders to a stop.

"Wake up." Ashley shakes my shoulder. "We're here."

"Are these the Catskills?" I'm stomping through the woods behind her. "Where are we, Ashley?"

"Shh. This way," she says. "Follow me."

We hike for what feels like hours through the darkness. Ashley holds a flickering lighter over her head. I clutch the hem of her blouse. We get turned around many times and twice lose the trail completely, and Ashley twists her ankle and we decide to rest for a while, but in the early morning we step out into a bright sunlit clearing. A windowless church, blackened from a fire, looms before us.

"I think this is it, Tom," she says.

"Todd," I correct her.

"Anybody here?" she calls out.

A barechested man in canvas shorts and muddy work boots strolls out of the church wiping his hands on an old T-shirt. "Help you?" he says. His black-bearded chin juts out like a pugilist's.

Ashley announces that yeah, sure, he can point us to the commune, because we're prepared to give up everything, including the clothes on our backs and every penny in our pockets, to get away from the stifling and traditional bullshit of American corporate culture. We will work hard, eighteen-hour days if need be, to aid the community.

He laughs. "Well, well. This might be the right place for you then." He introduces himself as Dallas.

I hoist my hand for a high-five. "Todd," I say. "Todd Gronski. A pleasure."

Dallas leaves me hanging, then he sits us down on a rock like little kids at summer camp and explains to us how the community works. "And it does work," he says, eyeing me with suspicion. "If you want to be a part of this, friend, listen to how it works."

I'm still holding my empty highball glass in my hand. I lick the rim to get the last speck of gin into my body. "What makes you think I'm not listening?"

Dallas warns us that our per capita rates of consumption of non-renewable resources have to be close to nil. He expresses his concerns about soil erosion and trace mineral deficiencies and the unscrupulous use of artificial fertilizers, not to mention the disturbance of natural cycles of animal and plant life.

Ashley nods her head. "Totally, totally," she says, beaming at him.

I yawn. Yet another false turn. How can I possibly get my work done out here? The lighting is all wrong, for one thing. It's too windy. Too many trees.

Dallas points at the charred walls behind us. "This church was built in 1846 by disaffected Lutherans," he says. "We've held meetings in it twice a week for thirteen years. We're not a cult. We don't follow any particular religion. Whatever you want to believe is your own business. Like I say, this isn't a cult."

"Methinks the lady doth protest too much," I say.

"What?" he says.

"Nothing."

"Listen, man. We got cabins here," Dallas tells me. "Larry and I built them ourselves last spring. Four people to a cabin. How it works round here. Take it or leave it." He turns smiling to Ashley. "So we'd kinda prefer that you bunk up in them, instead of building anything new."

"No worries," she says and blushes again.

"Okay, cool." He claps imaginary dust off his palms. "Why don't I show you around?" Dallas guides us through the trees, swatting branches aside with his lean, powerful arms. Ashley stays close behind him. Dallas talks about a man's need for self-sufficiency. He tells Ashley about his own desire to escape America's deadly corporate fundamentalism. Ashley says she totally agrees.

Razor sharp twigs zing by my face.

"You, *Toad*," he says at last, "you go over there," pointing to a surprisingly nice-looking wooden bungalow. "You'll be bunking with The Stork, Anton, and Boris."

"Who?" I say.

Dallas laughs and disappears deeper into the woods with Ashley.

Seated on the wooden front step of my new home, a tall, ropy-limbed guy with a mulish face frowns at the tattered paperback in his hand. "Ever read Hawthorne?" he asks without looking up from *The Blithedale Romance*.

"Not that one," I tell him.

"Hawthorne had no conception of what real communal living is like." He closes the book. "Marcus Williams," he says and rises to his full height. His legs alone seem about six feet long. "But folks around here call me The Stork. I don't mind."

"Todd Gronski. A pleasure."

We shake.

Marcus rubs his glasses on the front of his tattered purple T-shirt. "So I see you met Dallas," he says. "We've had some undesirables out here lately, college students trying to dig up dirt for their little campus papers, so Dallas likes to test new-comers right from the get-go. But don't mind him. He's good people. One helluva harmonica player."

I sit down next to The Stork on the splintered step. "Pretty quiet out here," I say.

"Yup," he agrees.

A minute passes in silence.

"It's nice and all, tranquil," I say, "but I just worry that I won't be able to get any work done."

After five days I begin to pick up on patterns. A dark-haired woman named Francesca lives in the cabin next door to ours. She has a soft hoarse laugh that she isn't at all shy about. Every morning before dawn Francesca stands naked on her front steps and stares up at the sky. I'm always up early, too. Ever since I was a little kid, I've had trouble sleeping for more than six hours a night. I like knowing Francesca is awake with me. It's comforting. But her shocking and exquisite nudity keeps me from focusing on my work.

Mornings she chops wood in the sun, or she works in her vegetable garden. A thick black braid swings across her narrow back. Her lean muscles flex and flash in the sun. I lower my eyes when she walks by, even when she's in her cut-off denim shorts and tank top. Then I look up again quickly, hoping to exchange a meaningful glance, but it's too late. She has already passed.

As the days turn into weeks, self-doubt assails me. There's no good reason for me to be living out in the woods, crashing in a bungalow with three stinky-footed dudes who snore and fart in their sleep. The bodega is miles away.

Day after day it's dirt and rocks everywhere you look, in your socks, under your fingernails, in the food, and jammed in your underwear. My hair is greasy, my skin always feels wet. We eat brown rice and bulgur and dried apricots and vegetable curry for lunch and dinner. I have mad diarrhea. And there are mosquitoes everywhere! And I never see Ashley anymore. She does some kind of sweat lodge thing with the women in her meditation circle. She never comes by my place for a visit.

Late at night I sit crosslegged on the roof of my cabin. The wind whips my long, greasy hair against my face. Each night I vow to begin my work the following day, but something always gets in the way. Indigestion. Poison ivy. Usually I just sit up here for hours and think about these mountains, all alive, like sleeping stegosaurs. We stomp all over their backs. Human beings are selfish, disgusting creatures.

The whole idea of sitting around and drinking beer and checking Facebook and Twitter now seems pointless to me. When you're out here in the world, in nature, hearing the birds making bird noises, you have a different perspective.

One night The Stork calls up and asks if he can join me. He climbs up to the roof and tells me he's been watching me. I have an independent frame of mind, he says. I'm not a blind follower like a lot of the people in the community. I'm not a people-pleaser. He says a lot of lost souls come out here thinking they'll abandon the world of conformist doctrine, when, in fact, they're just replacing one structure of control for another.

"Uh-huh," I say.

The Stork talks about his blinding anger at the current administration in the White House. He lists all the ways that the President and his cronies have committed impeachable criminal acts.

After a brief silence, I tell him the truth. "I guess I was so focused on my work that I never had a chance to think very deeply about these issues."

"I hear you," he says. "I was the exact same way before I opened my eyes and ears to reality. But it's no excuse. Remaining ignorant of the issues does not absolve you of the crimes being committed in your own name."

"I guess that's true."

"Future generations will not distinguish between me and you and the secretary of state. This happened in our time, on our watch. And what did you do about it?"

"Not a ton."

"We're having a meeting in the church next week. I'd like you to show up." He leans closer. "Not everybody here shares our opinions on how to effect change in this country. Have you ever fired a gun?"

"No," I say.

"You'll learn. Good night."

After The Stork climbs down, I find myself meditating on life and death. I consider how each life is basically inconsequential, the briefest flash of light between twin darknesses. Death leans against a nearby tree, watching us, laughing at our petty concerns, and picking his teeth with a nail, saying, "Soon, soon."

The following morning, Francesca accosts me on the steps of my own cabin. She claims that I am brooding, antisocial, unfriendly, a non-participant in the community. What's my frigging problem?

I tell her that I'm shy.

"You're too damn old to be shy." She cocks her hip. Her pudgy belly peeks out from beneath her T-shirt. "Are you a man or a boy?"

"A man?" I say. "Definitely a man."

She grabs my hand and shepherds me around the village, introduces me to a dozen people, tells them I'm a nice guy. Francesca makes it her mission to get me more involved in the community. "This is Todd," she says. "He's morose and insecure but very friendly when you get to know him."

"What's up? What's up?" I say, hoisting my hand for high fives. "Guten tag, y'all. Right on. Solid. Solid as a rock."

"He's not comfortable in social situations," she says. "He overcompensates."

"Do I?" I ask her. I shut my eyes and quote William Wordsworth. "I wandered lonely as a cloud. That floats on high o'er vales and hills. When all at once I saw a crowd, a host of golden daffodils."

A few dudes shake hands with me, their wrists cocked back for the free-spirit clasp, followed by a quick hug and a forceful pound on the back.

"Welcome, man. Yeah, I've seen you up on the roof of your cabin."

"Tremendous view," I say. "I'm getting way spiritual up there."

"Right, right. That's cool."

"I'll tell you another thing that would enhance my meditation." I pinch my thumb and finger to my lips, toke on an invisible joint. "I'm ready to face that green-eyed demon again. Who's holding the dank buds, baby?"

"Excuse me?" a man says.

"You know what I'm saying." I grin at him. "The *dank* buds."

"Franklin is a lay minister," Francesca says, seizing my elbow. "He doesn't do drugs." She guides me away from him. "In fact, he's quite outspoken in his opposition to them. Drugs are an escape from our all-too-real political predicament."

"My bad, Frank," I say over my shoulder. "The American Indian first showed us the way to this particular spiritual path, and I'm just following their lead."

"Drugs are the scourge of modern American society," he says.

"Drugs are a problem, true," I say before Francesca pulls me out of earshot, "but I'm only talking about weed and alcohol and certain pills."

I feel wonderful socializing with the gang. Francesca's right. I have been brooding. I need to think less about myself—my own work—and more about others. Death can watch me all day long. That's his business, not mine.

The autumn winds come cool and dry and fast, ripping arid leaves from the tree branches. The smell of wood smoke and peat permeates the crisp air. At midnight the sky is a braided tapestry comprising many subtle shades of color. Yellow-gray, streaks of indigo and silver. I have never seen skies like this before. Down below, in the distance, a bright red light shines. With the foliage now all gone I can see this strange red light glowing, pulsing. I don't know what it is, but each night I meditate on it. I've decided it's some sort of manifestation of a higher power.

Every morning I bring Francesca little gifts, usually small sculptures that I've fashioned out of dirt and dung, or knotted figures made from twine. Sometimes I pick wild flowers and leave them on her cabin steps. One night she invites me in for a bulgur and brown rice casserole. Afterward, we drink hot tea together and talk until morning. Francesca's murmured agreements goad me into unabashed confessions. I tell her that I feel bereft much of the time, that I'm looking for a way into my life. She tells me private things, too: a DUI at sixteen, a nasty divorce in Austin, Texas. We talk about music, art, politics, past sexual relationships, dreams. In the past, when a new woman intrigued me, I would run the word MARRIAGE up the flagpole to see how it looked there, flying in the wind like the death's head on a pirate ship. But it doesn't scare me when I think about being married to this woman.

I wait, I watch, I plan my attack. Finally, I drop down to one knee in the dirt and say, "Francesca, let's get married. What do you say?"

She takes hold of my shoulders and brings me back to my feet. She calls matrimony an archaic system that demeans women and turns them into property. "I'm not chattel," she says.

I say, "Hell no. You're so much more than that."

But we compromise and decide to conceive and raise a child right here in the woods. We move into our own cabin and have unprotected sex many times a day. Thus begins the most wonderful three weeks of my life.

The Stork encourages me to show up at a secret meeting. "You won't be able to vote on anything yet, and there's a brief initiation," he explains as we approach the site, "but I'm not worried about you. Hell, we can use some fresh input around here. It gets a little incestuous after a while."

My old nemesis Dallas steps out of the church and lights a cigarette. He takes one look at me and blocks my path at the door. "Not him. Sorry, Stork."

"Why not?" Marcus says.

"This guy is not one of us."

"I can vouch for Todd."

"This guy?" Dallas asks him. "He's a poseur. Are you for real?"

"Real as the Captain and Tennille," I say.

Marcus puts his hand on my shoulder. "I'll handle this, Todd," he says. "Come on, Dallas. You're paranoid."

"I'm safe and disciplined. That's more than I can say for you."

"You don't have the final say in everything, you know. This is exactly the type of behavior we were trying to escape. And if we're really going through with this, man, we can't afford to be picky. We need all the manpower we can get."

Dallas stares at something just over our heads.

Marcus turns his discouraged face to me. "Listen, Todd," he says, but I wave away his explanations.

"It's cool," I tell him, and I walk alone back to my cabin.

"Secret meeting over already?" Francesca asks me. Smiling, she looks up from the bed, where she's reading a year-old *National Geographic*.

"You're beautiful." I join her in bed. "This is everything I need. This is the sum total of my rebellion."

"Come here, chicken legs," she says. "Hold me. Keep me warm."

The early months of Francesca's pregnancy are easy. She chops wood with the same inimitable fervor as always. And I pitch in where I can. One afternoon I even help Dallas pour cement for a new church foundation. I'm not getting my own work done, and at times I get depressed about that, but I try to convince myself, as most young fathers do, that this new responsibility—the family!—is much more important work. At night Francesca and I fall into bed together, exhausted.

After six months of pregnancy she's often winded and has to sit down on a mossy stump, her head bowed, breathing woof, woof. Now I chop all the wood while Francesca sits nearby, smiling and rubbing her belly and chewing on a stalk of grass. I make us dinner. I clean up around the cabin.

We survive the winter. Everybody in the village pulls closer during this time. We share clothes and food. Many of us struggle, including me, and some of us sulk for days and mock the entire enterprise (me again), but we do our best. When spring comes, we laugh easily and embrace our friends. Life seems glorious.

Then, to our horror, in the eighth month of her pregnancy, Francesca becomes seriously ill. Pale and clammy, running a high fever, she can no longer get out of bed. "Don't touch me," she growls. "I'm fine."

After examining Francesca with a homemade speculum and a penlight, Dr. Roderigo pulls off his yellow dishwashing gloves. Sighing, he invites me to join him outside the cabin, where we can talk in private. "Meconium in the amniotic fluid," he concludes. He places his firm hand on my shoulder and lowers his head. "I'm sorry."

"What does that mean?" I ask.

The moon looms above us like an enormous unblinking eye.

"The baby's pooping in its own food. That doesn't bode well, my friend."

Francesca loses the baby.

We're devastated. The entire village rallies around her, they are really supportive, but my Francesca is inconsolable. She locks herself in our cabin, refusing all attempts to help her. She tolerates me and allows me to share her bed, but I can see that even my presence makes her uneasy.

I sit crosslegged on the roof at night and seek answers from a silent higher power. Praying, I stare down into the dark swirl of rich evening colors. That's when that red light comes to me again. I stare and squint, bring it closer to my consciousness where I can translate the glow into meaning.

RED LOBSTER, the sign reads.

Maybe we are not so deep in the woods, after all. My mind empty of delusion and desire, I can now hear car engines and shouting voices. There's a honkytonk bar in the lot next to the Red Lobster. It's called the Make Easy. I can read its sign, as well. Mud-caked pickup trucks are parked in the gravel lot. I shut my eyes and feel the hot wind stabbing me through this beautiful poorly made sweater that Marcus gave me many months ago. I need to change my life.

Francesca gets worse and worse. Her sadness debilitates her. She refuses to accept that death is part of life. She talks about our stillborn child, calls it Bethany. Eventually she chooses to leave the community altogether and move back to her parents' house in Dearborn, Michigan. To regroup, she says.

There is a tearful ceremony on the night we decide to leave the village. Dallas speaks in glowing terms of Francesca's unselfish commitment during "the lean, early years." Everybody applauds Francesca. As she packs her things in our cabin, she says, "Stay in the village, Todd. You're needed here. This is your home now."

"I want to be with you," I tell her. I'm ready to leave at a moment's notice. I don't own much. A few dung sculptures. A leaf collage I've been working on. What have I accomplished in my life besides loving Francesca? Frankly, I'm a failure in everything but my relationship with her. The truth is I haven't gotten much work done out here. And so what? All I want now is that tame domestic life, the Volvo station wagon, the dinner parties with couples we both envy and despise, a front lawn that I hate to mow.

"You're not listening to me," she says. "I can't be with you right now."

I follow Francesca anyway. It's difficult, though. We are both hitchhiking in separate cars. Every time I confront her in a rest stop or a motel along the way, she begs me to give her space.

"Okay, you've forced my hand," I say in a Motel 6 parking lot. "I'll even give up my work for you."

"Todd!" she shouts. "Stop harassing me!"

A man unloading the trunk of his Buick pauses to watch us.

Harassing? I only want to be with her, to comfort her. But standing in that parking lot in a stinky communal sweater and another man's shabby trousers, I feel like a fraud and a heel. "Fine," I say to her. "Go!"

Still, I hole up in a motel just outside of Dearborn. To wait.

I need to regain the spiritual serenity I had once known in the mountains, on the roof of that cabin, but it isn't as easy down here in the city. Horns honk incessantly. Drivers shout at you. Babies shriek while mothers chat idly on cell phones.

To make my rent, I wash dishes at Wang's Clam Digger in east Dearborn. My boss, Henry, a heavily tattooed albino, wears a gun holster under his fringed leather jacket. Every day is fraught with anguish and insanity. And every night I attempt to contact Francesca. I send her Wang's discount coupons in the mail. I stand on her parents' moonlit front lawn, hoping to rekindle her dormant enthusiasm. "Francesca," I shout at her bedroom window. "You know I love you."

She says that if I don't go away, she will call the cops and have me arrested.

Entire weeks are a blur, a smear of vague memories. I wander across America, distraught, blind drunk most the time. I work countless part-time jobs. In Hellwater Springs, California, I'm known by some fraternity guys as Caveman. I sleep on the beach in my pissy trousers. They yell "Caveman!" and throw beer cans at me.

"I have work to do," I say, spinning around, throwing wild blind punches.

They drive away in their Lexuses and BMWs, laughing.

Even in despair I'm industrious. I return their empty cans and bottles, pocket the deposit money.

At night, an elderly woman named Lillian cuddles up next to me for warmth. Her breath is awful, bracing. A foretaste of death.

"Frosty . . . snowman," she sings softly in my ear.

I can't sleep without drinking myself into a blackout. My stomach lurches when I try to eat anything solid. Two of my teeth come loose; one falls out into the sand.

"I loved her like air, like food," I say. "I even neglected my work for her."

Lillian spoons her tiny body against me.

The next morning I wake up hungover, feeling humiliated even though I can't remember much from the night before, and it occurs to me that I need to go home. Brooklyn was never the problem; I had been the problem. New York City, I realize, is where I belong. New York City is where I will finally create a monumental work of Promethean ambition.

I hitchhike in cars, trucks, and vans. Our country is so huge and filled with wackadoos. A generous and violent coke fiend treats the last leg of my trip as a solo mission, charioting me from Bloomington, Indiana, without stopping. He plows ahead at an incredible rate, averaging somewhere between seventy-five and ninety miles per hour. His meaty hands strangle the steering wheel of his Dodge Charger. He snorts cocaine off the blade of a pocketknife while driving. I try not to look directly at him.

He drops me off somewhere in the Bronx.

"Thanks, man," I say to him. "God bless."

He rolls down his window and glares at me. "Fuck off," he says mildly. A gray cloud emerges from his mouth. He's too tired to put much venom into the insult. He has not slept much in the previous seventy-two hours. I know what that feels like.

I ride the 1 train to 96th, transfer to the 2, and sleep 'til Brooklyn, where I transfer again at Atlantic and get an R to 25th. There's a hard-packed ectoplasm of dirty, crusted snow on the ground. I see gray snow banked up on sidewalks and pressed high against the sides of buildings, clinging to the walls. The temperature is 11° F, according to a flashing sign outside a closed bank. My breath steams from my mouth. I feel my brow wrinkling and my jaws grinding. I'm home.

On Fifth Avenue and 19th Street, I slip and slide on the sidewalk. These borrowed shoes are three sizes too big. Inside the bodega on Molly's corner, I buy a twelve-pack of Yuengling.

"Raaaa!" A lean, bearded man lurches from a doorway and approaches me, his face swollen, darkly bruised around the eyes. "Raaaa!"

"Hello, Lucifer," I say and hand him a dollar. I have two in my pocket. "I told you I'd give you something."

"Oh," he says, looking down at the bill. "Merry Christmas."

"You too," I say. "Stay warm."

A brick props open the building's security door. I race up three flights of steps. "Hey, anybody home?"

Molly emerges from behind the yellow bedsheet that separates the kitchenette from the living room. "Popcorn," she says, holding up the bowl. "Have some, Todd. As you know, I only use real butter. The fake stuff, I've heard, causes cancer and liver damage."

"It's good to see you again," I tell her.

She holds out the bowl and rattles it at me. "Get it while it's hot!"

My numb fingers rummage awkwardly in the bowl.

"Oh, good. You bought beer," she says and kisses my cheek. "Whoa, Grizzly Adams, you might want to think about investing in a razor."

Her open laptop gives off its familiar blue glow. She sits on the futon and begins pressing keys. "These GMOs are really bad news," she says in a quiet voice.

She's still so beautiful.

The winter wind howls outside. Hail pounds at the windowpanes. It sounds like little kids are standing below and tossing pebbles at the glass.

NOTHING TO DO WITH ME

One morning over breakfast Milana told me about an old boy-friend of hers, Steven Trimm, who had self-published a chap-book of haiku. *Peripheries*, he'd called it. He carried dozens of copies around with him in a hemp shoulder bag and sometimes read his poems at open mikes and on street corners.

"He sounds like a jackass," I said.

"Well, I thought it was cool that he *had* a passion," Milana said.

At the age of twenty-three I was still learning when to speak and when to stay silent. It was a painful process. Even though I wanted to demean the guy some more, I decided to let it go. I wasn't going to let the ghost of this Steven Trimm character and his hemp sack get me into a pointless quarrel with my beautiful girlfriend. After all, Milana was living with me, not him.

"I agree. Here's to Steven," I said, toasting my orange-pine-apple juice. "Out on the periphery."

"You think everything's a joke, but for your information being an artist takes a lot of courage." Milana was a modern dancer and had many artist friends, whereas I was still floating around a year after college, working a dead-end job for the city. I kept talking about going to France but it didn't look like it would ever happen. "Being an artist also takes hard work and dedication," she said.

I knew that. But I wasn't going to bow down before a self-published haiku writer.

"Steven took his craft very seriously," she said. "Some people don't think making art is a great big joke."

My buddy Clay had recently taught me an all-purpose phrase that he said worked like a charm with his girlfriend. "You're right, honey," I said, reciting Clay's lines. "I am wrong. I was insensitive."

Milana just stared at me. "What's that you're doing?"

"What?"

"Are you imitating a robot?"

"No! I'm saying that you are right. I am wrong. I was insensitive."

"So you admit that it's difficult to write and publish a haiku?"

"I am sorry," I tried again. "You are right. I am wrong. Honey, I was insensitive."

"I think you're mocking another person's attempt to be creative because you're too scared to try anything like that yourself, and you're intimidated by people who do."

One thing about me: I loved a challenge. I said, "How does it go again? Refresh my memory banks. Five-seven-five, right?"

"Oh, stop. I'm not saying that I want you to—I love you for you, babe. I don't expect you to—"

"Five-seven-five." I'd taken a few English-lit courses in college. "No sweat. Any monkey could haiku."

Milana smeared apricot jam on her toast. "You're cute."

"You want a poem, lady? You'll get one. Tonight. Count on it."
She laughed. "Yeah?"
"Shake on it." I held out my hand. "Deal."

On my break from cleaning sidewalks that morning, I peeled off my sticky gloves, busted out my new ballpoint pen and note-pad, and prepared to write. I touched the pen's tip to the paper, so ready to write.

Nothing happened.

Not a problem, I decided. Inspiration didn't come all at once, I understood that, but you had to become willing to receive it. I kept the notepad in the back pocket of my work pants for the rest of the day. Every now and then I made ready to compose, my pen poised over paper. "Fat cloud in the sky . . ." Five sylla-bles. A start. It was tricky, because I had an inborn disdain for any type of structure, and haiku was nothing if not structured. I put the pad back in my pocket.

My coworker, James, a tall, dark-skinned man in his late thirties, walked ahead of me with his dustpan and broom. Every now and then he turned and observed me from behind his mir-rored sunglasses with a sort of vague anthropological interest. One of his favorite phrases was "White folks crazy."

James shook his head in mild reproach, and his out-of-fash-ion Jheri curls glistened in the sun. All the other black guys on our crew had shaved heads or close-cropped hair. They taunted James, called him "Dripmaster Flash," but James never both-ered to respond. He wasn't their friend; he wasn't my friend. He just showed up to do his job. He wasn't there to play the fool. Our boss, a balding white sadist named Mike McCloskey, left him alone. James carried himself tall, even when he was drag-ging four dripping trash bags across the street.

Meanwhile, now that I had embarked on my new avocation as a poet, the twenty-block stretch of Main Street, which I had patrolled blindly for months with a pan and broom, appeared new and interesting. For once I was really looking at what was going on around me. I saw pigeons strutting Mick Jagger-like on cracked concrete. I saw three winos, gap-toothed and debonair, chatting on a junked lavender sofa under a skeletal maple tree. I saw a pink gum blob, melted on the sidewalk skillet, clinging in long delicate strings to a fast-walking businessman's wingtips. I saw Korean hot dog vendors playing Chinese checkers on a rickety card table between steaming grills. Fast-talking merchants sold purses, watches, jewelry, shea butter, hot sauces, and jerk spices. The books for sale ranged from *Soul on Ice* to *Wretched of the Earth* to *Pimp: The Story of My Life.* Cosmic orange flyers for weaves and extensions swirled around one's feet, promising 100 PERCENT REAL HUMAN HAIR!!!! I lingered in the clouds of African violet and sandalwood incense smoke, browsing the bootleg VHS tapes from blockbusters still in theaters.

By lunchtime I felt like I was seeing the world afresh. The break room offered a choice of reading materials: *USA Today* or nothing. I hunted for poetic material in the Life section. Twenty minutes into my lunch hour, I put down my slice of pizza and wrote my first full haiku:

> Priest on a blanket
> asks the new kid to join him
> for a slice of cake

James didn't think much of it—"Hmnpf" was his review—but that didn't discourage me. This first haiku opened the floodgate. Within minutes I wrote another, and another. They were not good, but it didn't matter. I wrote about pigeons and street people and stray dogs and politicians and the Middle East. By 2:00 I'd written a dozen.

Most of these poems, thankfully, have slipped through the loosely woven net of my memory, and the notepad has not survived my many abrupt and ill-advised moves, but a few haiku still remain fresh in my mind, the ones that seem to drift toward grief. One of Milana's gifts to me, I realize now, was the daily example of her kindness. She wasn't even all that tolerant, but she had me beat by a mile. Despite all my posturing and bravado, I was just a sheltered kid from a provincial town who found it easier to mock everything than admit ignorance and ask for clarification.

That afternoon James and I drove a hundred wet trash bags to the dump, where a private waste management company would cart them off the next day. I rode shotgun and scribbled poems while James leaned out the driver's side window and said, "You're doing it, angel," to women in power suits; "You're doing it," to college girls in short shorts and to the Jamaican queens in their bold floral prints; and, mixing it up a bit, "Keep on doing it now," to the hippie chicks in their long peasant skirts who sold incense, homemade jewelry, and Lebanese hash out of their Army surplus duffels.

Somehow this wasn't considered creepy. Most of the women seemed to take it as a compliment. I have since tried to say, "You are doing it, angel," to a few ladies, and I wouldn't describe the results as successful. Some men can chat up strangers with style and charm, and some men cannot. This was James's own original catchphrase, spoken so many times in my presence that it sounded as familiar to my ears as "Hello" and "How are you?"

James flirted with more women in an hour than some guys do in a month. He flirted with women in wheelchairs, women in passing cars, nuns in habits, and one outpatient whose head was in halo traction. He didn't care, as long as they were female and in the eighteen-to-fifty-five age range. I don't even think James was trying to get laid. He just liked to acknowledge their beauty.

"This is *my* time," James said, his eyes concealed by his wraparound shades, his right arm draped over the steering wheel. "Summertime, summertime."

"Mine too," I said. "I like the scenery."

He nodded. "Nice scenery," he said. We drove on to the dump.

The job had been decidedly less utopian during the winter months when, instead of pans and brooms, James and I had carried snow shovels. Our backs ached as we trudged through snowdrifts wearing hooded parkas, waterproof gloves, and rubber boots. During February in Buffalo, a man's thoughts sometimes turned to suicide. Attractive women still walked by us while we tried to get warm in a vestibule of the Main Place Mall, but James remained silent. Once I said, "Hey James, you missed one. Didn't that 'angel' warrant a 'you're doing it'?" and he told me to stop running my mouth. It was the only time he ever snapped at me.

The melting month of March seemed years away.

Even in winter, though, we owned the street. Sometimes we were more like policemen, James and I, than sanitation workers. We knew all the homeless people and kept up with the feuds and rumors. We knew that one old man had Alzheimer's or some form of dementia, so we didn't hold it against him when he pissed on the tram tracks. We knew that Laurel traded sex for drugs. One of the other guys on the crew, Tareq, once told me that Laurel was in her late thirties, but I refused to believe that. She looked sixty.

"Hey there, Tareq," Laurel would call out in a coy voice. "Why you ain't called me?"

She teased all of the sanitation guys, trying to provoke or embarrass them.

"You left your wallet in my bedroom," she said to James once, who just walked by her in silence.

"Some sad shit right there," Tareq said, shaking his head.

Laurel inspired one of the few haiku I still remember:

A rotten molar
she spits from her mouth and coughs
clutching a gin flask

Sometimes I'd sit beside her on my smoke break. When she was drunk or high she babbled and growled and gesticulated with her dirty hands, the words unintelligible, her yellow-and-blue eyes glassy and raw, but occasionally a name or a place would bubble to the surface of sounds—Dolores, Chicago—and I'd attempt to piece together a narrative from the clues she'd dropped. I imagined that few people, if any, took the time to listen to Laurel, so I made an effort to sit with her whenever I could. Dolores, she said, Chicago, she said. She smelled bad, though, like rotten eggs. I held my breath and tried to conceal my discomfort when she touched my hand. She asked me if I had a girlfriend. I told her all about Milana. My girlfriend was an artistic, brilliant, no-nonsense asskicker. I loved talking about her, partly because the relationship bestowed upon me a glamor or mystique I hadn't possessed before. Laurel said, "Hold on to that one." I wished her a good day and walked away thinking Dolores, Chicago, Dolores, Chicago. I was twenty-three years old. Whose name, I wondered, would remain on my lips after everything else had burned away?

On the snowy streets James and I walked side by side. Occasionally I hung back, let James get ahead of me. He never turned around, always kept moving forward, his shovel balanced on his shoulder. More than once I snuck into the mall, hotfooted it to TGIF, shook off my coat, and slammed down a couple of beers at the bar. James never said a word to me, and he never ratted me out to McCloskey, as far as I know, but it now shocks me that I could have been surprised by James's occasional chilliness with me. What did I expect? Even though I was a loafer, I think I assumed everyone would give me respect, whether I'd earned it or not.

The homeless needed far more help—medical and psychological—than we street sweepers and snow shovelers could offer. On a gray February afternoon, James and I came across a stabbing victim lying on the sidewalk. Somebody had plunged a flathead screwdriver into the man's chest. I took a knee and tried to calm him, but he writhed and squirmed so much that I couldn't do anything. I had no medical training. Still, I put my hand on his shoulder, said, "Relax, relax, relax," thinking he should try to remain immobile, calm his breathing, not tighten up in the cold.

James said, "Don't get that man's blood on you."

A crowd formed around us. The ambulance would take forever to come because of the snow and traffic, and the police were nowhere to be found. For a long minute we all stood around like catatonics, the orange light from our truck's beacon flashing across the dirty snow.

Finally James said, "Fuck this. Grab his legs."

I hoped he wasn't talking to me. As much as I wanted to help the guy, I'd also heard that one shouldn't move an injured person. Everybody knew that.

He definitely was talking to me, though, because he said, "Hey, Slim," which was the nickname our boss, McCloskey, had bestowed on me. I was a tall, gawky kid, all rib cage and elbows, and I hated that nickname because only really scrawny or superfat guys were ever called "Slim."

"Grab his damn legs, Slim."

"But it's a crime scene," I said. "Shouldn't we wait for the cops?"

"Come on now," James said. "Move."

Against my better judgment, we hoisted the shrieking man into the sour-smelling bed of the pickup truck, where he lay between the bloated black garbage bags, and James drove fast through a lace curtain of falling snow.

Beeping the truck's horn and yelling out the open window, he fishtailed into the parking lot. After they wheeled the man into the emergency room, James parked the truck on the street and killed the lights. We stared out the windshield, watching the snow fall and listening to each other breathe.

"If it's a choice between letting him die or moving him," he said, "you move him."

It sounded like he was rehearsing his speech to McCloskey. We were not supposed to take the truck out of our jurisdiction—ever.

"Right," I said. "The guy stops breathing, us moving him is the least of his problems."

"You can't hurt him worse than dead."

Later we heard that the man had pulled through his surgery, and we were famous for a day. Some of the homeless sneered when they saw us shoveling—"Look out, it's the good Samaritans"—but James ignored them, and I followed his lead. We cleared a walkway and continued on, business as usual, and I thought about how James had acted the night before, with no concern for lawsuits or prevailing wisdom. He just hit the gas, ignored all traffic signals, and saved a man's life.

We all took abuse for doing a job that nobody in his right mind would want, but as one of the few Caucasians on foot patrol I took an extra dose of scorn.

> "White boy, why you here?
> Urban renewal? Naw, man:
> Negro removal."

Only James seemed unaffected by taunts and slurs. Day after day, I worked beside him and ate with him at Burger King and Pizza Hut, but he was one of the most private men I'd ever met. When the other guys talked about football, food, and women, James wouldn't join in. I knew nothing about his life except that he had a daughter. I was just a coworker and this was just a job he did to keep the electricity on.

> walked five miles today
> trash swirling on street corners
> same as yesterday

James's other signature phrase was "Ain't got nothing to do with me." He said it so often, in all situations, that I sometimes tried to get him to say something else just for variety's sake. Once, on a warm day in late March, when drops of rain were hitting the windshield, I said, "You think it's gonna rain today, James?" thinking I'd get him to laugh and call me a fool.

But he just shrugged and said, "Ain't got nothing to do with me."

I pushed the issue. "But what are the chances of precipitation today, would you say? Fifty percent?"

He stared dead ahead through the wet windshield. "Ain't got nothing to do with me."

At the time I decided he was speaking philosophically, that in James's view only God had dominion over the world. Made sense. Of course a man shouldn't try to control what was not in his power to control. It occurs to me now, though, that he probably went home that night and said to his wife that rain was smacking the windshield clear as day and he's stuck with some crazy-ass white boy asking if it's going to rain.

We never learned his wife's name. He refused to speak it in front of us. None of us had earned that privilege.

We spent a lot of time together in the truck. A rare smile sometimes curled at the corners of his lips, even when he tried to suppress it. Once, he burst out laughing when I frolicked across the street, carrying two trash bags in each gloved hand. Slyness burned beneath his silence, but the answer to most of my questions was always the same. "That ain't got nothing to do with me."

I have since wondered if I could have gotten any closer to him—that is, if I didn't have such a crap work ethic, or if I didn't reek of beer in the morning. Befriending me wasn't worth his while, and I'm sure he knew, long before I did, that I wouldn't last longer than two years at that job. He had seen my type before. But it wasn't just me. James refused to make friends with anyone there, even though he'd been on the job a decade or more. That independence made him seem more powerful than any of us, McCloskey included.

On the day I wrote poems for Milana, I asked James to stop at the liquor store. "I'm having a little get-together at my place tonight," I told him. "Nothing special. You should stop by. Milana would like to meet you."

"Go on in the store," he said, taking off his sunglasses and rubbing his eyes.

"Really, you're invited," I said. "We'd love to see you there."

James looked through the windshield.

I ran into the store and bought two handles of vodka and a fifth of rum.

Dolores cried out:
Where have you gone, my sister?
We're in Chicago.

"I was out on the street the other day, looking for you," McCloskey said in the shop. "Did you go into the mall for something?" He stood by the time clock and manipulated his face into a smile. "You can tell me. A lot of them do it."

"I was in Friday's," I said, pretty sure he already knew the answer. "I drank a beer."

He nodded. "You're an honest kid," he said, displaying what passed for a smile, a toothy gash overruled by hostile eyes. "Who knows? Stick around here long enough, you might have my job when I become executive director."

"Hmpf," I said.

"And James drinks on the job too, right?" McCloskey said, nodding his head to invite agreement. "Hell, I don't care. Who wouldn't? He does, right?"

"Nope," I said. "Never."

"Hah. Loyal, too. Wouldn't you like to get off the street, son? Get inside with a better class of people? I can put a word in for you."

"James doesn't drink on the job. Ever."

"So much better to be inside where it's warm." Crew cut, muscular neck. A tyrant in a clearance rack suit. "Find you a desk and a comfortable chair."

"That ain't got nothing to do with me." I gave him a huge fake smile that matched his own. "And by the way, I quit."

"Excuse me?" he said.

"I quit."

He laughed in my face. "You serious?"

"Dead serious."

Both hands on his stomach, McCloskey let out the guffaw of a hammy thespian. "What a terrible loss to the company. How will we ever continue without you? Street sweepers are so hard to train."

Tareq passed behind me, a stealthy shadow moving along the wall. He couldn't escape McCloskey's gaze, however. "Hey! New haircut, new attitude, huh, Tareq? Is that a fade? Can't wait to see you out there on the street today with that new fade. Bet you'll work twice as hard, huh?"

Before I punched out, I took one last ride to the dump with my partner. We had to dispose of a broken toilet from the shop. I told him I wouldn't be riding shotgun anymore. Getting away from McCloskey would be a nice change, I said. He was such a racist asshole.

James said nothing. Half an hour later, he parked outside the shop and left the engine running.

"Hey, you should quit, too," I said. "That'll show him. Really, you could do so much better than this. You should be *his* boss."

James gave me a look that was different from his usual head shaking, a look that implied I really was incurably insane, that my decisions had nothing to do with him.

"You going, or what?" he said.

My shift was over.

We shook hands. His utility gloves were on the dash, mine in my back pocket.

"See you soon," I said, believing it.

That night Milana and a half dozen of her dancer friends congregated in the kitchen while my beer-gulping buddies watched the hockey playoffs in the living room. Bottom lips pooched out like apes, they spat tobacco juice into empty beer cans and shook their fists at the TV screen. Though I'd known it would be risky mixing Milana's friends with mine, this was worse than I'd imagined. My buddies were beer-bloated ex-jocks. They were really intimidated by Milana's artsy-fartsy friends. I wondered what James would have thought of this divided assemblage: men in one room watching ice hockey, women in the other room talking about the movement of their bodies. Really I knew what he'd have thought, knew the exact three words he'd have used: *White folks crazy*. And I had to agree with him. There *was* something wrong with us.

All night long I moved from kitchen to living room, an emissary bringing the news from one world to another. At some point in the evening Milana found the notepad with my haiku in it and showed it to her friends. I heard the girls read each poem aloud and laugh, and then they cheered when I entered the kitchen. I couldn't tell if they were mocking me or not. Secretly I was proud of my work. I had never written a single poem before that day, and now I was the author of thirty-one. Maybe I would self-publish a chapbook and dedicate it to Milana. Or even to her ex-boyfriend Steven, who had done nothing to warrant my earlier disdain. I was just a jealous prick who envied and despised all Milana's other lovers, past and future.

It was a hot night. A dusty metal fan rattled on high speed in the open kitchen window. A stick of sandalwood incense burned a tear-shaped groove into the sill. The floor was sticky from spilled beer, but nobody cared. The dancers got drunker and drunker in the kitchen and discussed Rauschenberg and Merce Cunningham, "phrasing" and "partnering" and other dance topics alien to me, and I nodded my head and pretended to know what they were talking about. Then I joined the grunting apes in the other room and went wild for a bench-clearing brawl in the third period.

When the doorbell rang, I hoped briefly that it was James. I had a vision of him hanging out in the kitchen, standing a foot taller than the girls, holding a rum-and-Coke in his hand and disarming them all with his smile. I answered the door, ready to welcome in the guest of honor, but it was a pizza-delivery guy looking for my neighbor's apartment.

After the hockey game ended, my buddies immediately herded down the stairs and drove drunk to Regan's Backstreet Bar for the Tuesday night beer special: five-dollar pitchers. If it weren't for Milana, I would've been at Regan's with them, squinting at the dartboard and drinking Hamm's from a plastic cup.

The dancers relocated to the now-vacant living room. Milana cranked up my stereo, tied a red scarf over the ceiling light, and everybody danced. Nine months later she would leave Buffalo and move to New York City, but on this night in late May she danced toward me, rolling smoothly across the hardwood floor, languid and effortless, her joints like greased ball bearings, her hips doing things that I can't even describe. As always, I wanted to hide and felt like I didn't belong in this world with these people, but every time I tried to sneak away, embarrassed, Milana pulled me back into the center of everything.

"Where do you think you're going?" she said. "Dance with me."

And I did, even though my moves were stiff and the results were pretty comical. But the women weren't watching me. They were immersed in the music, in their physical response to the music, and none of them bothered to register my insecurity. Milana smiled and danced, her joy coming from somewhere other than her mind.

This ain't got nothing to do with me, I thought. Just move, Slim.

And it worked. On a blood-pink night in Buffalo, New York, surrounded by women whose names I no longer remember, I danced like a happy idiot for an hour, grinning and flapping my arms, blessed as any human being could be.

THE ECSTASY
OF BIOGRAPHY

1.

The biographer must be a sort of bifurcated animal, digger and dreamer; for biography is an impossible amalgam: half rainbow, half stone.
— PAUL MURRAY KENDALL, *The Art of Biography*

She was born in Akron, New York, in 1971. As a child she played alone in a dirt lot behind her family's wooden farmhouse, hacking the synthetic hair off her dolls with left-handed scissors. "Naughty," she said, shaking a new doll in her fist. "You are bad bad bad." She drenched the doll in kerosene and set it on fire, her narrow face glowing in the flames. Standing behind the wooden fence, picking our noses, we watched her.

We called her the Artist. We were not much older than she was—Clive was the elder statesman at eleven—but we recognized genius when we saw it. Judging by the confident way she leaned against that fence, picking her scabs and spitting into the dust, we knew that someday she'd be famous. And each one of us wanted to be first to write her unauthorized biography.

When she was nine, metal braces were clamped on her teeth to correct a slight overbite. She did not open her mouth in public for an entire month. I attempted to write a chapter about this pain and alienation, entitled "Her Angry Silence," but there really wasn't enough to hold a potential reader's interest.

In 1981, she broke her left leg in an accident. We were immensely encouraged. She crashed her cousin Darryl's go-kart into a tree. That evening I scrawled in my journal: "Her tibia snapped like a breadstick." I was thirteen and had just invented similes. I liked them a whole lot.

But many years passed without any further notable incidents. The Artist attended Akron Middle School, played a passable clarinet in the band, even auditioned for the lead in *Anything Goes*, losing a close battle to Traci Lynn Baxter, a spirited soprano.

Her collected homeworks from this period (1982–1984) revealed little originality or depth of thought. The letters she wrote to her grandmother in Sarasota, letters we intercepted every year, were marred by careless repetition, as though she had merely plagiarized earlier efforts. "I miss you so much, Grandma. I hope to see you soon." It was disappointing stuff.

"After such a promising beginning," Celia sighed. "Have to admit I'm disheartened." Her acne-speckled face flared with indignation.

In 1987, the Artist's father was relocated to Buffalo, forty miles away. *The Boon Years* is how we like to think of them. To our parents we explained that we, too, had to move to Buffalo. At first, they were skeptical and understandably combative, but they came to recognize the truth: We had been called to a vocation.

We packed our bags and rejoiced. "It's a new beginning," Celia said, filling her suitcase with stuffed giraffes. Even Clive cracked a thin grin. In short time, just as we'd hoped, the Artist—alienated, lonely, and eager for acceptance—fell in with "the wrong crowd" in the densely populated Buffalo public school system. Boozing, pot smoking, unprotected sex, etc. We sharpened our pencils. We prayed for an unplanned pregnancy or venereal disease.

"The clinic looms like a citadel over our dreams," I wrote one chilly November morning, still delighted by similes. "Dark days barrel towards us like a DeLorean at dusk." Alliteration came into fashion in late 1987. I applied it pathologically to every punchy paragraph in my journal.

We snapped covert photos of the Artist walking through the city of Buffalo, admiring her spiky red hair, ripped jeans and combat boots, that delightful bullring through her septum.

"We're on the precipice," I said, and scribbled possible chapter titles in my journal: *Wilderness Years. The Rise of the Phoenix. Stand Back!*

Unfortunately for us, her rebellion manifested itself only in her attire. In every other way, she was levelheaded and conventional, alas, a B+ student who volunteered at a tutoring center after school.

We waited.

Wet snow clumped down on our heads like spitballs from God, winter after unrelenting Buffalo winter. We huddled outside her favorite coffeehouse. She never read any poetry, only listened and clapped politely. Each morning we trudged out of our small apartment on Niagara Street; and every evening we returned, empty-handed and demoralized.

Our families recognized the supreme importance of biography, of course, but it would be inaccurate to say they never worried about us. I worried about us. The apartment we squatted in had no phone, no electricity. We began to resent the Artist. It was misleading to appear rebellious and creative, and yet be bland as skim milk. The more we dug into her vanilla personal life, the more we worried about our future sales. Couldn't she at least break something or, better yet, get arrested? For months we followed her to punk shows in VFW halls and musty basements. We saw a great deal in these places. Dyed hair. Piercings. Tattoos. But it was all so much cosmetic angst, the lowest form of defiance.

When a man bumped Clive in the men's room, Clive turned a critical eye on him. "Sorry, hoss, but your little tattoos don't make you an outlaw," Clive told him. "You simply paid to sit in a chair for twelve hours while somebody painted on you. Congrats! Good use of your chump change."

The man had to be restrained.

We left the VFW hall shortly after we realized that nobody at this show was going to make art, including the musicians onstage.

"Dammit, I'm going to find a new artist," I threatened one night at the Old Pink Flamingo. "One who *produces*."

The others ignored me. We were in too deep to turn back—of course I knew that!—and it was too late to choose another artist. We were stuck with her, as she was stuck with us. I went home and stared at my stacks of notebooks, filled with nothingness.

But then one morning, when all seemed lost and my existence an utter waste and ruin, the Artist and I exchanged words for the first time. In my journal I refer to this as *The Turning Point*.

"Hey man, that's my bike," she said, bursting out of the Lexington Co-op with two recycled plastic bags swinging from her fists.

"Oh, sorry." I dismounted. I had simply wanted to feel what it was like to sit where she sat. She glared at me as she pedaled away. "Next time I'll call the cops," she said over her shoulder.

The experience transformed me. I burned my journals and everything else, the half-finished chapters, the immaculate Prologue, the eye-catching opening lines, everything. I called the other biographers to an emergency meeting. "Guys, I have a radical idea. You ready for this?"

"Spit it out, Brendan," Clive said.

"Why don't we make our *own* art?"

The others fell silent. Benoit whistled low and turned his head. He had obtained a one-year work visa, which he kept referring to as a *carte de séjour*. He didn't understand what I meant. Neither did Don, who grumbled into his beer.

"Look," I said, "what we're doing is not fair to the Artist. We started with good intentions, but let's be honest, this pursuit has become more about us than about her. Our egos are involved now."

Clive jabbed his index finger into my solar plexus. "Ridiculous," he said. He branded me a hack journalist, a charlatan, a poseur. "You're the one holding us back, Brendan."

I could hear the voices of my compatriots behind us: "Drive him from the fold, Clive."

Somebody grabbed me from behind, pinned my arms behind my back. Another biographer kicked me in the ankle.

Celia put a stop to the attack. She told them to let me go. "Maybe you don't have what it takes, Brendan," she said to me. "Maybe you aren't really an unauthorized biographer, after all. Only you know the truth."

I panicked, fearing another attack. Where would I go if I lost my community? What would I do?

"Hey, I was just testing you guys," I lied. "To see if you were up to the challenge." Then I related the bicycle incident to them, embellishing it with strong emotional conflicts, mythological references, Good vs. Evil, Innocence vs. Experience, all that. "I wasn't trying to steal her bike. I thought it might fuel her creative juices, you know, challenge or inspire her. I did it for inspiration. I did it for Art, yet she has produced nothing, despite my efforts."

The others watched me closely. "What?" I shouted. "What?" In one motion they all looked away from me.

2.

On the trail of another man, the biographer must put up with finding himself at every turn: any biography uneasily shelters an autobiography within it.
  —PAUL MURRAY KENDALL, *The Art of Biography*

The Artist is now twenty-eight. She works at a bagel shop on Grant Street. I have been battling depression, though I am against taking medication. The best and most timeless art is borne (they say) by struggle. This unauthorized biography I am writing will be the Boswell of its class, or at least the *Diana: Her True Story*. The others have lost faith in me, but I don't care. Proust went into his cork-lined study and nobody knew what he was doing. What am I saying? They don't know what I'm doing? Or do they know what I'm doing? What if they are watching me? What if this interest in the Artist is merely a front for a more insidious surveillance? Are they secretly writing tell-all biographies about me? They are diabolical, fiendish, are plotting to kill me, and they must be stopped! That's absurd. They're my friends, my closest allies in the fight against lies and misrepresentations. I will continue on, as normal, for now.

Each morning we huddle together, watching the Artist through the bagel shop's front window. The red and brown leaves swirl around our knit-capped heads. We blow hot breath into our cupped hands and rub our palms together. I'm wearing all of my shirts.

"She's spreading the chive cream cheese," Evelyn whispers into a handheld recorder. "The customers appear to be pleased with the amount. She doesn't gunk it on too thick, but she's not stingy with the stuff either."

"Masterful." Clive nods in approval. "It's a statement piece. She's pushing the boundaries by making the ordinary extraordinary."

But these moments of enthusiasm are rare. We have become despondent, and many of us have turned to the insidious pleasures of drink. "We're all going to hell anyway," Don says, sipping bourbon from his thermos. The sun is out today for the first time in months, burning carrot-orange in a hazy white sky, and despite the chill there is a spirit of rebirth in the air. Behind me, the others scribble notes into their pads or whisper excitedly into tiny tape recorders. I cannot help but think they are talking about me.

At closing time, the Artist takes out the bagel shop's garbage. We scramble for cover, diving behind parked cars.

Later that night, I rifle through the trash bags searching for clues she has left behind. Her work does not move me deeply, but I believe close scrutiny of the material might reveal something enlightening. I shove a sodden tea bag and half-eaten ginger cookie into my coat pocket, new evidence that I may or may not share with my compatriots. I am dying to be present for what I'll later call *Her Breakthrough Years.*

In the morning I wake up to find that the ginger cookie has been stolen from my pocket. The teabag remains where I left it, having thoroughly soaked through the fabric of my pocket. I study the impassive faces of my colleagues, pacing back and forth before them, scanning their chests for crumbs or granulated sugar. Who has stolen my research materials? My guess is Don.

A shocking development interrupts my investigation: Evelyn bursts through the door and reports that the Artist is visiting the Albright-Knox Art Gallery. We mailed her a free pass last week. We pile out of the apartment, hop on our bikes, and ride across town.

The Artist shows little interest in contemporary art—the bulk of the gallery's collection—but the Impressionism hall seems to pique her interest. We tiptoe behind her, scribbling notes, murmuring into our voice recorders. Not without reason, I hope that she will go home and start sketching, her fingers blackened with charcoal. I close my eyes and consider the possibilities. But the worst possible thing happens, an event we could not have foreseen: She meets a young man in the gallery's café and they chat for well over an hour.

When the Artist hands him her phone number, we nearly leap up shrieking "No!" from our corner table. A casual romance artificially assuages a young artist's hunger to create. We must drive a wedge between them.

Her apartment is tiny, just one room. She lives alone. Two windows and a hardwood floor. Futon, stereo. The usual. Lamps, candles, incense. Sometimes Dave, the guy she met at the gallery café, comes over with a twelve-pack and spends the night, but mostly she sits around in her bathrobe, drinking coffee or watching TV.

"The television again," Benoit whispers down to us. He's standing on our shoulders, his nose pressed to the glass. "Always the television."

"What's she watching?" Eduardo asks, pen perched over his notepad. It is 10:30 at night. A coal miner's lamp affixed to his forehead shines down on the page.

"Don't know yet," Benoit whispers. "It's a commercial."

"Is she creating any fucking *art?*" Gunnar asks. He's been living off a grant from the Swedish Coalition for Contemporary Art for fourteen years now. His patrons are demanding to see a product soon.

"*Non,*" sighs Benoit, shaking his head. "But now she's . . . Hold on, she's clipping her toenails."

"Moving from the largest toe to the smallest?" I ask, shivering in anticipation. "A gradual recession in size, a sophisticated system that might suggest—"

Benoit shakes his head. "*Pas du tout.* She's clipping one of the middle toes. She started with a middle toe, if you can believe that."

"Innovative," Gunnar says. "Groundbreaking."

"Describe her posture to us." Celia looks up from her notepad. "This could lead to something."

Benoit presses his nose to the glass. "Well, she's got one foot up on the coffee table," he says, "and she's kind of hunched over. Wait. This is interesting. There is a bowl of ice cream on the table."

"Flavor!" Don shouts, stomping around on the fire escape. "What's the goddamn *flavor* we're dealing with here?"

"Shhh, Don," we hiss at him. "Relax."

So many nights pass like this. We lose parts of ourselves out here beneath this brilliant white moon. I vaguely remember my early childhood. Sometimes it comes to me like light exploding from a Kodak flash. Oh, how I loved to crouch behind trees, mailboxes, and old dogs. I felt both a part of the world and protected from it. And I relished peering through a keyhole as my parents attempted to conceive another child, a sibling for me to study. They tried without success for months but one had to admire their innovations.

As the Artist moves from one room to the other, Benoit narrates the action. "Ah, *putain,* she's shutting it down for the night," he says, and rakes his hand though his hair. "Who wants to watch her undress?" Nobody takes him up on the offer. We have seen it all before.

I am awoken from a standing dream when the Artist flings open her bedroom windows and shouts: "What the hell do you people want from me?" Her eyes are swollen and unattractive. "Why do you hate me? I don't understand."

We're shocked by the question. We love, revere, *adore* her. And yet the truth is our job would be much easier if she were dead. A tragic accident, I hate to say it, would increase her appeal. But she is so damned careful.

We drift off to sleep on the Artist's fire escape, our legs and arms entwined, a many-headed animal of biography. At 3:00 in the morning, Jim Sheehan, a popular local novelist, rides his rickety ten-speed bicycle on the street below. Sheehan's well known in Buffalo for his so-called "dirty realism": spare, minimalist narratives about earnest blue-collar workers.

Personally, I take issue with the concept of "realism." What is that? Realist for whom? Its practitioners and adherents are far too concerned with appearances, in my opinion, to engage the full complexity of modern existence. Any literary work, including one that pretends to a realistic sketch of life, remains an artificial construct. Only the absurd gets close to an adequate depiction of the berserk experience of being alive. Why waste your limited time on earth skimming the surface of the appearance of consciousness?

"Real art had the capacity to make us nervous," Susan Sontag argues in *Against Interpretation*, and I'd go even further than that. A work of art must dislocate me, wound me, force me to reevaluate my positionality. If it doesn't, if it leaves me unmoved or complacent, then the artist must be destroyed.

We carry rocks in our pockets expressly for dirty realists like Sheehan. Gunnar heaves a sharp one. The minor writer ducks his head, pedaling much faster now. Celia hurls a hunk of concrete into his spokes. Sheehan spills over the handlebars. The bicycle clatters on the pavement.

"Police," Sheehan shouts. Down on one knee in the street, he presses his hand to a bloody gash on his forehead. He kneels like a penitent in the posture of prayer. "Somebody help. Call an ambulance, please, the cops. I'm hurt bad." He looks up at us. "What the fuck? Why did you do that?"

Don laughs. "How you like that for reality, tough guy?" He descends the creaking iron steps of the fire escape. "Come on," he calls up to us. "Are you with me?"

We don't have to be asked twice.

We run down and pounce on Jim Sheehan, pulling his hair and kicking him in the face, ripping his clothes and pummeling him until he says no more, until his eyes close, until nothing remains in the night but silence, and the sounds of us, only us, breathing hard.

PLAYING PING-PONG WITH PONTIUS PILATE

In the YMCA sauna, Bill Drucker, a pharmacist, was holding forth on the subject of mutual funds, pros and cons, when the door banged open and an icy blast of air slapped everybody's cheeks and chests. Pontius Pilate strode in, his wool robes shushing against his naked hairy ankles. "Hello, boys," he said. Father Delmont, who was seated next to me, cinched his towel at his waist and left the sauna. Pilate insinuated himself between Drucker and me on the wooden bench and tapped my knee with his white-taped fingers. "I have been looking for you," he said. "We're on at three, my friend."

He was referring to the YMCA table tennis tournament. Earlier in the day, I had been loitering at the bulletin board, eager to see who I would play in the third round of the tourney. When the results were posted, I shuddered at the name of my opponent.

"Tough draw," said Brad Thomas, reading over my shoulder.

In the cramped sauna, it was hard to ignore Pilate's presence. He shook his thin body out of his robe and cozied up next to me. The stale stench of athlete's foot and musty wool assaulted my nostrils. Humming what sounded like "Good Day Sunshine," Pilate ladled water over the hot ceramic rocks. "Warm enough, my friend?" Greasy mustache hairs curled down into his mouth. His bearded face was sharp and narrow, like an ax blade covered in moss.

I ignored him. Sweat rolled down my cheeks in the diabolical heat. "Talk to Ed Ramos about those mutual funds, Bill," I said to Drucker over Pilate's head. "He'll tell you what's what. He's a financial advisor, I think."

Pilate nodded. "That," he said, "is an important job. I was once the governor of Judea. Thankless work, all in all. But it had its perks." He smiled. "I sentenced people to death on a whim, things like that. But I find ping-pong a much more soothing activity, don't you? Of course, one must retain something of the executioner's calm concentration to be truly effective. See you at three." He strolled out of the sauna, whistling a dirge.

Bill Drucker mopped his shiny dome with his towel. "What the hell is that getup—a Halloween costume?"

I laughed. Pilate was an odd number, all right. But we were all deranged in one way or another.

"They should revoke his membership," Drucker said. "He creeps people out."

Two other members, both seated behind us on their towels, joined the discussion. "But what if it's not a role he's playing?" one of them said. "I mean, what if he's really the historical Judas or whoever?"

"You mean Pontius Pilate," the other said. "The guy who sent Christ to the cross. Don't you know anything?"

"So sorry I'm not caught up on my Bible homework."

"Guys, hey, take it easy," I said, turning to look at them. "Don't worry about Pilate. I'll beat him."

As the reigning champion, I felt pretty good about my chances. But Pilate was formidable in his own right. Nobody really knew what he was capable of. I had to admit, I was worried about facing him.

We were scheduled for table one in the Tony Carlucci Memorial Room on the second floor. In the locker room, I reviewed all that I knew about my opponent's style. Pilate used an unorthodox variation of a Korean penhold grip. His forehand was crisp and accurate; his backhand confident, reliably defensive. He would commit very few unforced errors. He was patient, calculating, and cruel.

What can be said about Pilate's footwork? Occasionally, in a tough match, he used a lateral crossover technique that seemed all but impossible in his heavy robes. When performed properly, the crossover is the most graceful way to cover four feet of floor space quickly. Crossing one dusty sandal smoothly behind the other, Pilate could move from the backhand corner to the forehand corner in the blink of an eye. In short, he had an all-around game. No weaknesses.

Most guys wore lightweight shorts and T-shirts. It could get awfully hot during summer, and there was no AC in the main building. But Pilate didn't seem to register the heat. He always dressed in wool robes and sandals. His dirt-encrusted toes (jagged yellow nails, never clipped) poked out from beneath the frayed hem of his robe. An adversary could not monitor Pilate's legs for clues as to which direction he might lean on his returns, and he often baffled his opponents with cross-table winners. We'd all heard the rumor that a dress code would soon be instituted banning strange and unconventional attire from match play, but I argued against it. We didn't need to start discriminating, I said. Where would it end? Surely the weight and hang of Pilate's vestments counteracted any advantage he received from them. No matter how you sliced it, though, he was a tough opponent.

I had two hours to kill before the match. I sat by my locker and tried to pray, mouthing the words I'd been taught in rehab, but I felt foolish and hypocritical.

At Hurley House, they told us to get involved with activities, to stay busy, and to say a prayer when we felt squirrelly. Go to meetings. Make phone calls. Don't sit around and waste time, they said. My mind was a dangerous neighborhood, they said, and I was supposed to stay out of it as much as possible. I joined the YMCA the day after I got out of Hurley House. The Y was perfect for me, a place I could go during the day, a place to hide. Within a year I had mastered most of the group activities. I've always been good at games. Ping-pong pleased me in a way that not many other things did. I enjoyed the repetition of it and could get lost in its rhythms. I stopped obsessing about drugs and alcohol. I made some friends. Started to look people in the eye. Every night after work, I took the bus to the Y. Ping-pong, in some ways, became a religion to me.

At one minute after three, Pontius Pilate bustled into the Carlucci Room with his duffel bag slung over his shoulder. He was a wiry little dude, short in his sandals, and he exuded an aura of self-destructive confidence. The pungent smell of chlorine and cherry cough drops wafted behind him. "I need to stretch my limbs," he said and dropped his duffel by the humming Coke machine in the corner. "Or are you in some big hurry to begin?"

The mind games had already begun. He knew the match was scheduled to begin precisely at three. He was attempting to determine my threshold for frustration.

"Fine," I said. "Do what you gotta do."

He winked at me. "Thanks, babe." And he launched into a ferocious display of violent kickboxing and tae kwon do maneuvers. "Hi-ya! Hi-ya!" He punched and kicked the air. Then he segued into light aerobic exercises—"One, two, one, two"—twisting his torso from side to side. "Busy day in the pool," he said, and dropped to the floor. "Newborn babies and their dads." He pulled each thigh to his chest, counted to seven, then released. "Kids under the age of twelve should not be allowed in a pool. They urinate." Pilate scissored his hairy legs above him, his hands on his hips. "A little chilly outdoors, eh? Supposed to be sunny today. High of seventy." He leapt to his feet and turned his back to me. As he bent over to touch his toes, he flipped aside his robes and addressed me from between his legs. "Ever read the Gospel of John?" he asked. "A fair assessment of my role in history. I found no fault in Jesus and attempted to release him."

"Hey, man," I said, "no more theatrics. Are we gonna start soon or what?"

He held up his wrapped index finger. The soiled adhesive tape was sweaty and unraveling. Jagged edged, it still bore the teeth marks where he had bitten it off. "First things first," he said and bowed his head. "Let us pray to Jupiter." After what appeared to be some form of silent meditation, during which his lips moved quickly, he peeked open one eye and grinned at me. "Ready?" he said.

I nodded, stonefaced.

We volleyed for serve. He won and held the ball up for me to see. "Pontius Pilate to serve," he announced.

The match was finally underway.

Pilate hit with remarkable power. I noticed that he changed his grip on almost every serve to prevent me from anticipating his next move. He grunted over every swing. The ball came fast and high, taking me by surprise. Serves blew by me. "That ball is gone," he said as I chased the ball halfway across the room. "It was banished, driven from the table. Gone: like religious faith, like romantic love, like an unattended plate in a Chinese buffet."

Once he got rolling, it was hard to shut him up. Pilate was a master shit talker.

"Under certain circumstances," he said, blinking at me, "can a rock be both igneous and sedimentary?"

I said nothing.

"I think it can," he said.

Still I said nothing.

We played without speaking for six or eight points. Pilate calmly flicked his wrist to return my serves, singing quietly to himself: "*Hot blooded, check it and see. . . .*" The ball kept coming back at me. "*I got a fever of a hundred and three.*"

No matter what I threw at him, hard or soft, he returned it. Pilate was a "reactor." He recognized all variations of spin. He was savage with my short serves, merciless with side topspins. If I stood back too far he would drop a short underspin return just over the net, where it would die quivering. If I crowded the table, he'd bounce a high smoker into my sternum.

The score was 12–8, Pilate. Ball in hand, he swayed over the table, taunting me. "I am going to serve now. But where will it

go? Nobody knows. Look out. Could be hard, could be soft."
He lurched forward, grunted, and served up a short sidespin
that slid off my end of the table like a cube of Jell-O.

"Thirteen for me," he sang, "but only nine for you."

"Eight," I said, low.

"Oh, right. *Eight*. You're so honest. How commendable."

"Just serve the ball and stop yapping, old man."

"Heavens, am I bothering you? Terribly sorry." And he
rifled a quick serve into my abdomen. "Fourteen," he said.

I battled back and won seven consecutive points. The ball
streaked over the net, a flash of white. Soon I had him on his
heels. He committed his first unforced error. "Christ," he said.
At 17–16, my lead, with the momentum clearly in my favor,
Pilate cried: "Ow, wait, I stubbed my toe. Time out," and he
hobbled over to a nearby chair.

He sipped a plastic cup of water and fanned a towel in
front of his face. Grimacing, he twisted his foot up and closely
inspected his filthy, wrinkled arch. A minute passed. I refused
to show any reaction. Rubbing his toes, he smiled at me and
said: "Let's get to know each other a little better. Okay? These
tournaments are always so impersonal. I'm Pontius. And what's
your name again?"

"Nick."

He squeezed his big toe. "Pleased to know you, Nick. Are
you Catholic, by any chance?"

I knew I shouldn't answer, but I did. "My parents were," I
said.

He nodded. "Funny how Catholics have such a burning
desire to embrace Rome, although Romans were their greatest
persecutors for centuries." He kneaded his toes. "Ever been to
the Vatican? Jeezum Criminy, that's a sight, huh?"

One thing was clear: he would stop at nothing to defeat me. He hoped to make me question my faith right there in the Tony Carlucci Memorial Room. But I didn't have any faith—none that I was consciously aware of, anyway—so his little salvo missed its mark.

"No more talk." I headed back to my side of the table. "Time's up."

"If that's how you play the game, Nick." He winced. "My foot really hurts. I think it's swollen. But if you cannot allow me another minute of rest, I understand. I shall limp over and try to compete."

I didn't reply. Pilate remained seated. He rubbed the sole of his foot.

"I'm curious," he said. "Do you like me?"

"Aw, man. Give me a break."

"It's a reasonable question. Theologians portray me as reluctant and weak." He looked up at me. "By vilifying me, they neutralized the conflict between the early Christian Church and Roman authority. They knew they would have to iron out their differences eventually, and they needed a scapegoat. *Et voilà. C'est moi.* I'm the fall guy."

It made sense, but I didn't want to think about it. I wanted to win the match and continue on to the quarterfinals. I wanted to keep going to my meetings, climb the ladder at my job, marry a woman, start a family.

Pilate lowered his eyes. "You know, I am a person too, Nick. And I have made some mistakes, but . . ." He waved his hand. Sniffling, he turned his head. "Sorry," he said, rising unsteadily to his feet. He came over to my side of the table. "My mother passed away a few years ago, you see, and I moved here for work last year and haven't made a lot of connections yet. Do you know what that feels like, Nick, to be so alone in the world? Won't you be my friend?"

For a moment I was tempted to console him, but I remained silent.

"What was your childhood like, Nick?" He had not yet picked up his paddle. He leaned his right hip casually against the side of the table. "I'm interested. You can tell me. I promise I won't tell a soul."

I examined the paddle in my hand. "It's not important," I said.

"Don't worry. I know all about it. And I want to help you, Nick. The question is, will you let me help you?"

In Hurley House, they told us to seek a higher power— meaning anything greater than ourselves—to stay right sized. My sponsor said I could live a rich spiritual life without pledging allegiance to any particular religion, but I needed to find a God of my own understanding. At first, it sounded like a load of hot steaming crap. You want me to build my own God like some kind of divine Dagwood sandwich?

But what were the alternatives? My best thinking usually landed me in the holding center or the emergency room. For years I'd looked for God in bottles and books and women and sex. None of those options worked for me.

I sat through our daily meetings in Hurley House with my arms crossed on my chest. Couldn't they see that I was not one of them? But every day I listened to others talk about their higher powers, and I became envious. Anything that helped me get outside of myself and become useful to others could be considered a higher power, my sponsor told me. Trying to diminish my ego, I mopped the floors and took out the trash. I made my bed every morning. And I waited. God never cradled me in his smooth palm and stroked me like a beloved pet hamster, but one morning I woke up and did not hate everybody and everything I saw.

"Are you considering my offer of friendship?" Pilate's chapped lips parted to reveal a warm generous smile, the smile of a kind uncle. It confused and frightened and intrigued me, but I knew the ways of manipulative men. They had been my teachers, and I had become one of them.

He spun the paddle in his hand. "Did you learn my name, Pontius Pilate, in Sunday school? Did they talk about me quite a bit? I bet they did."

"You're going to be okay," I said to him, trying to be compassionate.

Pilate let loose a huge laugh. "Oh, I know what you're trying to do," he said. "You want to be a more spiritual person, yes? A responsible, caring, *sober* adult. It's part of your recovery, this spiritual awakening. Is that not what you were told? I know you better than you think, Nick, you bad boy. Listen to me. They are lying to you. AZnd deep down you know they are lying. They tell you to find a God of your own understanding, but how can you have a religion, or a God of any kind, along with this burning anger? You want to let it out, and it must come out."

"Enough," I said, scraping my paddle on the edge of the table. "Let's play."

"*Let's play*," he echoed in a vicious voice. "Oh, I'm sorry, make way for the only person in the whole world. His majesty, King Baby." He glared at me. "Dammit, I know you, Nick. Hell, I *am* you. You live for the buzz you get from acting out—drinking, sex, gambling—but you can't sit with your feelings, can you? We're getting to the Core of Nick and you can't handle it, can you?"

I steadied myself against the table. If I attacked him, I would be disqualified. If I remained silent, he would think he'd rattled me.

Pilate stroked his beard with his filthy thumb and forefinger. "You were a terrible embarrassment to your family for years, Nick. I have heard many stories in these corridors, but none sadder than yours. And you think it's all different now? Your parents died, one after the other, before you could reconcile with either of them. You stole so much from them. You betrayed them. But how can you make amends with dead people? It's too late, Nick. You missed your chance."

"It's my serve," I said.

"No," he said and waved his hand, flourishing the white ball. "It is not."

He bounced the ball once, twice on the table. His hand closed over it. "The death of our loved ones is traumatic, Nick," he said. "Perhaps a drink would take the sting away. You pass a dozen bars every night after work. Who would know? No harm in one cold beer. Is there?"

And he served.

We battled back and forth. Winners, volleys, and unforced errors. We were tied at twenty-one, tied at twenty-seven. My wristbands were drenched with sweat. My thin T-shirt clung to my back. I lunged and skidded around the table. The soles of my Adidas squeaked on the polished hardwood floor. *Tok, tok, tok.* The ball flew over the net.

For a moment, Pilate held the ball and watched me with a mocking smile on his face. "Nick," he said, "please know that I want to help you. I'm *here* for you."

I looked up at the plaster swirls in the water-damaged ceiling. The custodian had done a nice temporary patch job but he'd left the crumbling sheetrock foundation untouched. The whole thing would have to come down eventually.

"I'm curious," Pilate said. "Do you take wine at Communion?"

I wanted to pound the living shit out of him. He was a confused little man in a reeking Salvation Army bathrobe. I could have easily slammed him to the floor. But I wasn't going to give him the satisfaction.

"Tired?" Pilate asked. He looked dry, rested, self-assured. Barely winded.

"No," I said. But I was. I had never felt so drained.

Smiling, Pilate opened his mouth and revealed a clutter of stained, crisscrossed teeth. "There's no need for us to be so competitive, Nick," he said. "Some night we should go out for a few beers and perhaps a fish fry. How's that sound?"

"Not interested."

Pilate was hiding inside his body, peeking out at me. His teeth were like cracked pottery shards wedged into his gums. I imagined yanking him out of himself with forceps and dragging him to a mirror. I wanted him to stare into his own weathered face. I almost felt sorry for him until he sent a spinning corkscrew serve into my abdomen when I wasn't looking. "Heads up," he said. "Stay alert."

We continued to trade points back and forth. When the score climbed to 31–30, my lead, Pilate dropped his paddle on the floor. "I see a hairline crack," he said, bending over it. "I'm afraid we'll have to suspend the match." He extended his arm to hold me back, even though I had remained where I was. "Don't touch it, Nick. We need to get this paddle analyzed by an outside panel of judges."

"Pick it up," I said, remaining where I was. "This will be a good lesson for you."

Pilate pouted and kicked the leg of the table. "You have no idea what it's like for me," he said. "God doomed me to walk the earth for eternity, engaged in mindless activities with fools. I come to this Y only to be ridiculed and—Don't you see? I did all I could for Jesus Christ. I did all I could for mankind. Read the Book of John. I did not want him to die."

"That's a sad story," I said. "Get ready."

"Look at me, babe," Pilate said. "I'm a mess over here. I picked up this awful robe at an Amvets. Even the drifters in Judea wore better threads." He clasped his hands before his chest as if in prayer. "Have mercy on me."

I bounced the ball on the table. I liked to believe that I thrived under pressure. "Pick up your paddle," I said.

"I'm sorry for how everything has turned out in your life," Pilate said. "I know you're suffering, Nick. I can see it on your face. Your pain rides shotgun when you drive, pushing your passenger up against the door."

I bounced the ball on the table. "Pick up your paddle," I said again. "I'm about to do you a favor."

In Hurley House, a guy named Florida Frank, a "graduate" who visited us weekly to share his story, told us that he performed one act of service each day. He wouldn't let his head hit that pillow, he said, until he'd done something good, however small, for somebody else. He'd open a door for someone, or he'd send an email saying he was thinking of someone, or he'd listen to a sponsee drone on about his problems when all he, Florida Frank, really wanted to do was watch the damn TV. Hey, he said, this was a small penance for being such a selfish prick for so many years.

Many nights I lay in bed thinking about what he'd said. Had I done anything that day, I wondered, to make life a little better for someone else? The answer, more often than not, was no.

I thought a lot about heliotropism, how plants turn toward what keeps them alive. How amazing! How natural! The majority of human beings probably do the same, but there are some of us—and for a long time I counted myself among them—who stubbornly refuse to take in what we need to thrive. And then we get to say, "Look at what the world has done to me," though we have done it to ourselves.

"Let's quit together." Pilate stepped around the table and stood beside the net. "We'll both walk out. A double forfeit. I'll buy the first round at the bar."

The desire to lose on purpose, to burn my whole life down again, was still so alluring. The hardest drug to kick was righteous indignation. *Look at what has been done to me.*

"Go back to your side of the table," I said. "Pick up your fucking paddle. Don't make me say it again."

Eyes lowered, Pilate did as he was told.

"My serve," I announced, and I held the ball up over my head. "Match point."

He clutched his paddle with both hands. "You can't win," he said, getting into his stance. "I'll rip you apart, kid."

Pilate was stubborn. How much longer could he hold out, furious and resentful at the world? Ten thousand years? Until he couldn't even remember why he was so angry in the first place? I doubted that he would ever be honest with himself. He whined and sulked like a child. He pointed his finger at everyone but himself.

To what lengths would he be willing to go to change his life? That was up to him. I could only share the most hard-earned lesson of my life, the idea that was only just then finding its way into words.

"You have to earn forgiveness," I said, and served up a beauty.

RETIREMENT HOME

Ryder carries a slop bucket of grub out to his parents. He unlatches the clanking gate of their chain-link cage and sets the bucket down in the dirt. Dressed in hip waders and a black winter coat with a fur-lined hood, he leans against the doorjamb and smokes a menthol cigarette. Overhead the sky has turned dark, overcast. It looks like rain again. Before he serves the meal, he sprays down the previous day's mess with a garden hose.

"Good morning," his mother says.

With a sharpened stick Ryder stirs the corn chowder. It was hot a minute ago, bubbling hot, but now it's lukewarm. He hoists the ten-gallon bucket and pours the chowder into their red plastic bowls, sploshing it over the sides so that it mixes a little with their water bowl.

"Your mother is speaking to you," his father says.

Crouched in the corner of the cage, his parents hug each other for warmth. It must have been cold last night, but Ryder didn't feel anything. He had his electric blanket cranked to 6. Toasty.

"I didn't sleep all that well," his mother says to him. "Your father and his snoring."

"That wasn't me, dear. Must've been your other husband." The old man grins at the punch line of a family joke.

"See you tomorrow," Ryder says and turns back toward the house.

They wave to him.

"Good seeing you, son," his father calls out.

"Thanks for visiting," his mother says. "The chowder looks wonderful."

His folks built this cage themselves. Nobody's making them stay inside. One morning Ryder and his little sister, when they were still small children, found their parents in this contraption. Ryder's sister cried and begged them to come out, her little fingers curled around the galvanized steel of the cyclone fence. Like penned animals they grunted back at the child, unable to make themselves comprehensible. Fine. Nobody gets a perfect childhood. But when Ryder caught his little sister building her own cage next to theirs, a sad structure made of wire hangers and twigs, torn linen, paper clips and doll hair, he felt responsible for her future.

Now he handles the daily feeding duties only after he has walked his sister to school. She is not allowed to play in the backyard when she returns.

Wet leaves and candy wrappers have blown against the east side of the cage and have clogged up several of the diamond-shaped apertures of the chain-link walls. Inside, the two grownups stagger across the dying grass, stepping over the jagged shards of green glass embedded in the dirt. There was a time when Ryder allowed them the privilege of a wine bucket and a case of beer, but after one too many incidents of violence, he had to cut them off. It was for their own good. During the first days of this prohibition they rebelled and pouted, but in time they came to recognize the wisdom of their son's decision.

Each morning Ryder sits in the gazebo and drinks hot chocolate from a purple ceramic mug. He's almost fifteen years old. He smokes three or four cigarettes and messes around on his laptop. From here he can monitor his parents' activities to make sure they're not hurting themselves.

A snapped branch of lightning brightens the sky beyond their house. Ryder looks into the distance. He feels a shudder beneath his feet, he thinks, though he knows this thunder must be coming from above.

"Another bucket, son," his father shouts. "Please. It won't be like last time."

"Get your own damn drinks," he says to his laptop.

Cold rain slants through the open roof of the cage. Ryder zips his coat to his neck.

His mother's eyesight has grown weak. Too proud to admit her failing, she pretends to have perfect vision, even as she trips and tumbles into the chain-link walls. She lowers her face to the chowder bowl, and sniffs. "He's become such a good cook," she says.

"Thanks, Mom!" Ryder says without looking up from the screen. "It's dump-and-stir mostly. Nothing fancy. I'm really getting the hang of that old crockpot, though I haven't mastered your bread maker yet."

"He's a fine boy," his father says. "You did a terrific job raising him. Best damn mother in America."

She lowers her head to the corn chowder and takes a tentative lick. "Could use the tiniest dash of salt, I think."

"Should I try to get his attention again?"

"Oh, no. He's very busy." She wipes rainwater from her eyes. "He's doing important work on that computer."

"Hey, Mom, have you seen the chewable vitamin Cs?" Ryder shouts from the gazebo. "There was a big thing of chewable vitamin Cs but I can't find it."

A gray strand of hair has fallen loose from her barrette. Her husband reaches out and brushes it back. "There's nothing I like better than eating a fine meal with you, darling," he says.

"Join me, my love." She pats the muddy floor beside her. Her beige nylons are gritty, torn. "Let's share this first entree and save the other for later."

"Good thinking," he says. "Winter's on its way."

They say grace in unison, their eyes shut. Then they lower their heads and devour the food their son has prepared for them.

BEFORE THE BURIAL

She was holding the stepladder for her husband when he fell. He'd climbed all the way up to the third rung. "Careful," she'd told him, "careful." Then he appeared to let go. She watched his fingers peel away from the aluminum—there was no other explanation, really—but everything had happened so fast, who could say for certain?

Sprawled on his back in the grass, he stared up at her, stunned. "I think I'm dead, Jane. Killed in a heroic plummet. Dead at seventy-four."

"Well, if you're dead, then surely I'm dead too." She knelt beside him in the grass. "Oh, we're dead!"

He tapped her knee. "Focus on *my* untimely demise, please."

"We're dead!" Jane ripped up clumps of grass and flung them into the breeze. "Oh, we're dead, we're dead. I never saw it coming."

Martin and Jane Warner found retirement challenging.

So much time to kill.

While she refilled the birdfeeder and scattered peat moss in the garden, Martin reclined in his armchair and daydreamed about nautical disasters. While he whisked eggs and shook fat sausages in a pan, Jane worked her crossword puzzle at the kitchen table. Minutes ticked off the clock. And yet somehow it was still always eleven in the morning.

After his tragic fall in the backyard, Martin shuffled and dealt a hand of blackjack at the breakfast table.

Jane had a king of hearts showing. "Hit me," she said.

"Are you planning to look at the other card before you make that decision?"

She picked up the cordless phone and dialed the Adamsons, their next-door neighbors. "Hiya, Barbara," she said. "How are you? Will Séverine be visiting you and Frank again this summer?"

"What are you doing?" Martin said and dealt her another card. "We're in the middle of a hand."

"Oh, shush, you. You had better sit down, Barbara. I have something awful to tell you. Marty died today." With the phone cradled between cheek and shoulder, she listened and nodded and sipped her iced hazelnut coffee. "Yes, I know, dear. It's devastating. He fell picking plums from the tree in the backyard. Plums! The old donkey weakened, and then I weakened. We're both on the fritz. Tragedy, comedy, who can say?" Cupping one hand over the mouthpiece, she pointed to her cards and mouthed, "I'll stay."

Martin flipped a card for himself. "Jack of hearts," he said. "The Christ card."

"No, it's not a sick joke. We're dead, Barb. I'm sorry to be the one to have to tell you this, dear." She flipped her cards over. "Seventeen. Barbara, I know it must be hard for you. Anyhow, the funeral will be on Friday. Spread the word."

Martin said, "Dealer has twenty."

"Rats." Jane smiled at him. "I should have taken a hit."

"You're not a real risk taker."

"Watch your tongue, Plum Picker. What, Barbara? No, he can't speak to you, dear. He's as dead as I am."

"Tell Barb I'm too damn busy composing our obituaries. These things don't write themselves, you know."

Jane Warner greeted the mourners at the funeral home's front door. "Thanks for coming," she said, squeezing hands, her face like a pearl. She wore a black high-collared dress with a fritzy orchid pinned to her breast. "So good of you to make it on such short notice."

Martin Warner stood on the opposite side of the room, dressed in a black wool suit and his lucky yellow socks, his black orthopedic shoes painstakingly shined. He shook hands with all the men, leaned down to kiss the cheeks of women he had known for decades. "Damned strange business, death," he said. "Hasn't really sunk in yet. Who will survive us? Who will remember us?" He looked wildly around the room. "Jane, my darling, where are you?"

She turned toward her husband. "You rang?" she replied in a deep voice.

"There are no grandchildren here to watch us die."

"Can I take anybody's coat?" Jane asked of nobody in particular. "I'd love to just hang up a coat or two."

Dozens of mourners sat with bowed heads, studying their programs and hunting for clues. They read every word at least once. Nobody said anything.

"A terrible mistake, not having sons and daughters," Martin Warner called out across the room. "My career, my career. Ptoo! It means nothing now. What was I thinking?"

"Soda, anyone?" Jane said. "Seltzer water? Can I make anyone a tuna fish sandwich with potato chips and a dill pickle on the side? I knew I should have prepared a funeral platter. A few pounds of prosciutto and melon—simple. Who doesn't like honeydew?"

Two coffins, gleaming like muscle cars under the bright ceiling lights, idled against the back wall. They sat atop pedestals draped in purple velvet. A day earlier, the Warners had picked out matching caskets under the supervision of the funeral home director, a sunburned man with a hyphenated name and a Florida-shaped birthmark on his cheek. "An excellent choice, sir," the man had said. "Bronze. Durable. Classic."

Martin Warner wasn't having any of that malarkey. "I am buying two coffins instead of one, so I expect a sizable discount on the second one, yes?"

The funeral director scratched his orange cheek with three fingers, producing a trio of fading white scars in the sunburn. "I suppose I can give you thirty percent off on the second one. A his-and-hers deal."

Martin Warner extended his hand. "Acceptable," he said.
They shook.

Jane squeezed her husband's elbow when they left the negotiating table. "You got him good, didn't you?" she whispered.

"I won that round," Martin said.

The mourners watched the Warners stroll down the center aisle to their bronze coffins. The old couple squeezed shoulders and shook hands, kissed cheeks. Good hosts to the last, they surveyed the crowd to ensure everybody was comfortable and lacked for nothing.

Jane lagged behind her husband. "Did you get your hair done, Colleen?" she said to a woman in the third row. "Looks terrific. I've been thinking about having mine frosted but I don't know if mine would—"

"Jane," Martin said.

"Coming," she called merrily. Then she stage-whispered, "He won't even be late to his own—"

"Jane! There is another ceremony scheduled after ours. Be considerate."

"Here I am!" she said in a loud voice, mugging for the audience. "Sorry to keep you waiting, your majesty."

"Oh, don't start," he said.

"Then don't finish."

The Warners turned away from each other and waved and blew kisses as if departing on a cruise. They smiled and laughed and posed for photographs that nobody took. And why shouldn't they have smiled, after all they'd been through? This funeral was a celebration of their long lives. They'd been fighting lately, true, and they still strongly disagreed on a number of issues, including the value and necessity of punctuality, but they'd been married for forty-one years. A touch on the shoulder, a smile—it didn't take much to reverse the tides.

"Janey," Martin said, taking her hands in his. "You've made me so happy. In sickness and in health. I give you my hands, my heart, and my love, from this day forward, until the end of time."

"Holy cow," Jane said. "That was really beautiful, Marty. I didn't know that we—I didn't prepare." She patted her hair with both hands. "Um, let's see here. Just have to wing it. How does that go again? 'Suntanned, windblown, honeymooners at last alone. Feeling far above par, oh, how lucky we are.'" She shook her head. "No, that's not quite right. 'Dum-dee-dum passing strangers now. Funny how things can change. We were so inseparable. Now you're acting very strange.' Wait a second, no, that's not quite right."

"I think that's enough, darling."

But Jane broke free of his grasp and belted out another verse, kicking her heels in the air. "There's no tomorrow when love is new! Now is forever when love is true!"

Never had a room gone more silent.

"It's time," Martin Warner said, tapping the face of his watch. "Allow me to help you, my darling."

As man and wife, they turned to face their coffins.

Martin supported Jane as she struggled to climb in. He pushed her upward, bending his knees to protect his lower lumbar. She hooked one pale leg over the side but couldn't seem to bring the other leg up. "I'm stuck," she cried, straddling the edge. She took a moment to admire the assemblage of her many friends. "Be well," she said to them. "Have a good weekend." She patted her husband's head. "I'm ready. Push me over, please."

Martin struggled beneath her, sweating. Two young men from the community rushed forward to help, but he waved them off. "I'm fine," he told them, and, harnessing all of his remaining strength, shoved with tremendous force. His wife toppled over into her coffin.

"Thank you," she called out.

Now that she was safely ensconced in the plush peach interior of her coffin, Martin Warner turned to face the mourners. The funeral was drawing to a close. Soon it would all be over: the minor triumphs and failures of his quiet life; the years spent alone in his downtown office; all of the birthday parties he'd planned for his wife; the unendurable retirement from work.

Martin glanced back at his own shiny bronze coffin, the lid open. It was as flashy and ostentatious as any new Cadillac in a showroom. The funeral home director—that slick sunburned bastard—had cashed in on a grieving couple's sorrow. It was so clear to him now under the funeral home's tawdry fluorescent lights.

"No, sir," Martin said in a choked voice. "That will not be the end."

He turned away from his coffin and embarked on a solo climb to his wife's resting place. The purple velvet bunched under his hands. His dress shirt was soaked through with sweat but he continued to hop and fall, grunting and cursing every time. One of his orthopedic shoes fell to the floor.

The congregation cheered him on. A rhythmic clapping ensued, rolling in waves from the back of the room to the front. "Go get her, Marty." "Don't let her get away."

He mounted the table, teetered, and caught his balance. He peered down at his beloved.

The room fell silent again. What could a man say at such a moment?

"For Christ's sake, Jane, do you have to take up the whole coffin?"

"What's wrong with yours? I bet it's got that delightful new coffin smell."

"Do I have to give a reason for everything I do? We don't need the other one."

"Let me move my purse then. Okay. I'm ready now."

The ceremony was almost over. Martin Warner wanted to say something wise and clever to everybody, give them a gift to take home, something that might ease their worries about their own aging. The clock above the door told the story. This room would soon belong to other people. A new generation of men and women, strangers to him, waited outside the funeral home. They would pay a hefty fee for this space.

He looked down at his bride, her petite legs crossed at the ankles. There she was: smart-mouthed Janey Paxton with that lopsided grin on her narrow mug, the stunning little pepperpot from Westchester, NY, looking like she'd seen it all before, even this, even this.

"Well, I'm waiting. You riding with me, Big Bear?"

Martin laughed.

He climbed in beside his wife and pulled the lid down over them both.

ACKNOWLEDGMENTS

Thank you to the hard-working editors, readers, and interns of the following magazines and journals where some of these stories first appeared: *The Sun, McSweeney's Quarterly Concern, McSweeney's Internet Tendency, Catapult, Southern Review, Okey-Panky, Electric Literature, Unsaid, North American Review*, failbetter.com, *Open City, PANK, Fiction International, Post Road*, and *SmokeLong Quarterly*. Thanks for believing that literary journals and small presses still matter to people, because they do.

Thank you to the bookstores I cherish most: Talking Leaves, Rust Belt Books, Housing Works, Mercer Street Books, The Strand, bookbook, Community Bookstore, Colgate Bookstore, Powell's, RiverRun, Skylight, and Square Books.

Thank you to my colleagues, friends, and students at Colgate University, especially Peter Balakian, Jennifer Brice, Brian Casey, Georgia Frank, Lesleigh Cushing, David McCabe, Matt Leone, Brian Hall, Lenora Warren, Ben and Katie Child, Susan Cerasano, Tess Jones, Hailey Elder, and Brendan Finn, and Katie Rice.

Thank you to the gentlemen at 107 and in Greenpoint for your humor and courage.

This book wouldn't exist without the enthusiasm of my fearless editor at Skyhorse/Arcade, Alexandra Hess, who laughs at the darkness.

I can't say enough about Lacy Lalene Lynch and Jan Miller, two immensely talented and dynamic women. Thanks to both of you for supporting and inspiring me.

Thanks as well to Kathy Daneman, whose humor and hustle made it all easier.

I am deeply grateful for the lives of SueAnn Ames, Stephen Ames, Kevi Ames, Stuart and Simon Ames, John Ames, Tina Lewis, Margaret Wooster, Marv LaHood, Tom Chapin, Peter Jackson, Deirdre Coyle, Max Rayneard, Josh Radnor, Neal Feinberg, Steve Haweeli, Hal Strickland, Bridget O'Bernstein, Jim Hanas, Snorri Sturluson, Virginia Zech, Mark Seemueller, Jack Cohen, Robert Axel, Suzanne Gorey, Lara McDonnell, Jack Vernon, Brent Birnbaum, Ian Caskey, Dave McInnes, Ed Carson, Clara Campos, Mat Lynch, Josh Carrick, Bill Walker, Deirdre Hayes, Jeff Oliver, and Michele Melnick.

Finally, this book is dedicated to the memory of Gus Vlahavas, my friend who ran Tom's Restaurant in Brooklyn with such grace and dignity. You are missed.

Greg Ames is the author of *Buffalo Lockjaw*, a novel that won a NAIBA Book of the Year Award. His work has appeared in *Best American Nonrequired Reading, McSweeney's, Southern Review, Catapult,* and *The Sun.* He splits his time between Brooklyn and Hamilton, New York, where he is an associate professor at Colgate University. He can be found at www.gregames.com.